A PLACE IN THE WORLD

DRUE HEINZ LITERATURE PRIZE

University of Pittsburgh Press

STORIES

A PLACE IN THE WORLD

Bill Gaythwaite

Winner of the Drue Heinz Literature Prize

This book is a work of fiction. Names, characters, businesses, organizations, places, events, and incidents are either the product of the author's imagination or are used fictitiously. This work is not meant to, nor should it be interpreted to, portray any specific persons living or dead.

Published by the University of Pittsburgh Press, Pittsburgh, Pa., 15260

Manufactured in the United States of America
Printed on acid-free paper
10 9 8 7 6 5 4 3 2 1

Cataloging-in-Publication data is available from the Library of Congress

ISBN 13: 978-0-8229-4876-6
ISBN 10: 0-8229-4876-1

Cover photo via Adobe Stock and modified
Cover and book design by Alex Wolfe

Publisher: University of Pittsburgh Press, 7500 Thomas Blvd., 4th floor, Pittsburgh, PA 15260, United States, www.upittpress.org

EU Authorized Representative: Easy Access System Europe, Mustamäe tee 50, 10621 Tallinn, Estonia, gpsr.requests@easproject.com

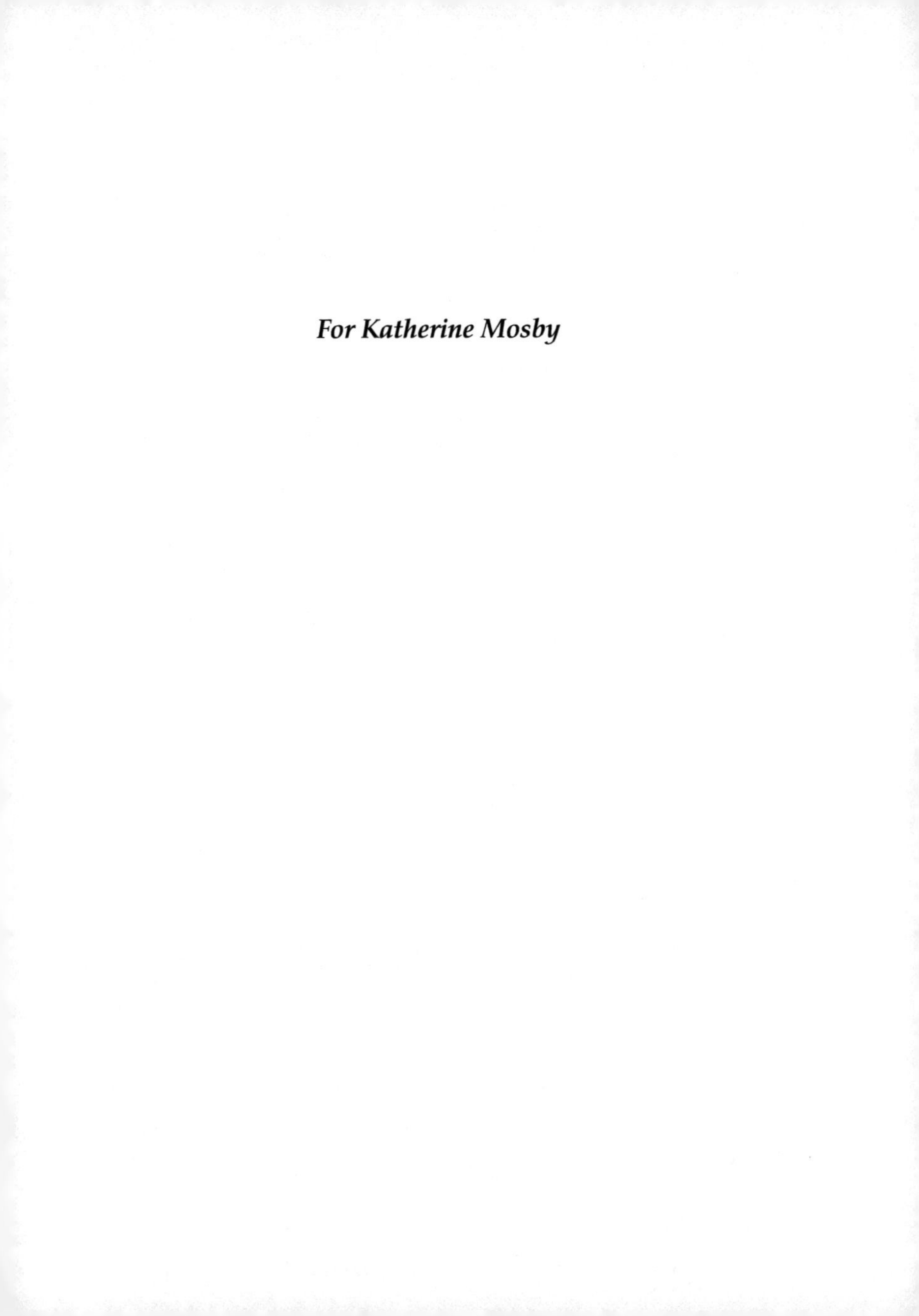

For Katherine Mosby

CONTENTS

A PLACE IN THE WORLD

A PLACE IN THE WORLD

I was getting some sun during my lunch hour the day I met Fisher. We were in the middle of Central Park, on that big green lawn called the Sheep Meadow. It was a warm afternoon in late April, and the sky had the pale blue look of faded denim. The park was crowded. The previous winter had been stubborn and miserable, like a houseguest who won't leave, so now everyone had been cheered by the nice spring weather. Wherever I glanced, New Yorkers were wearing expressions of gratitude and contentment. They didn't look like themselves at all. I was lying on the grass with my shirt off and my khakis rolled up above my calves.

"Won't you get itchy like that?" said a voice to my right. I propped myself up on my elbow and shielded my eyes from the sun. The man who was talking to me was seated on a blanket a few feet away, with a book in his hands. He had the round, plain face of a middle-aged infant and a look of weary politeness. All told, he was quite ordinary, like an extra in a crowd scene.

"You think I'll get itchy?" I said, in the bored, mirroring tone I often used at bars when talking to men like this.

"I mean to say, I have a towel that you can use."

And with that he produced and handed me one, which I took without even thanking him. I stood up, put the towel down on the ground, and sprawled out on it. Then I waited for him to ask me some more questions, which I planned to disregard. It was a way to spend my lunch hour. But he didn't say another word. This annoyed me. I turned on my side to show him my ass and then stretched a bit and flexed my biceps. I was twenty-four at the time, at the peak of my stretching and flexing powers. I wasn't used to being ignored. When eventually I caught him looking over, he gave me a prim, embarrassed smile. You didn't see much prim in this city, not in my experience, anyway. I was intrigued. I thought about my friend Buzz.

He would have called this "an opportunity."

I knew Buzz from one of my first temp jobs after I arrived in New York. We were in a word-processing pool at a law firm where all the senior partners had the dead-eyed stares of serial killers and the associates scampered around nervously like so many potential victims. Buzz was also my tour guide through the gay bars and clubs of the city. He was fun and campy and fond of using phrases like "A boy's got to take care of himself" and "Long live the checkbook romance!" He was the living example of such sayings, and now he no longer needed to temp, because he'd met a married doctor from Scarsdale who paid the rent on his little apartment near Sutton Place and gave him an allowance to buy ties and things at Bloomingdale's.

Before Buzz met his doctor, we would go out to certain bars in the city that he would laughingly refer to as elephant graveyards, because of the older, less desirable clientele. We'd let these old guys buy us some drinks and then we'd sit back, aloof and sneering, like royalty from a small country, while the rest of the evening passed in a blur of unspoken negotiation and a protracted tease. Buzz had actually found his doctor in one of these places, and I went home with a few guys I met in this fashion too, men who regarded me with the determination of hungry lizards, until they'd get me to their apartments, where they'd finally pounce, smothering me with their damp coughs and too much aftershave. As their hands traveled over me, I'd often will my mind to wander, like a runaway pet, and sometimes I'd disconnect entirely from myself and have something that resembled an out-of-body experience.

When I described all this to Buzz, he referred to the phenomenon as my "fugue fucks."

But other than being treated to a few expensive dinners or getting a knockoff Baume et Mercier watch or going away for a Hamptons weekend with a burly banker who wanted me to put him in a headlock while he recited German poetry, nothing much ever came of these liaisons.

"What are you reading?" I asked the man on the blanket. I was sitting up now. He looked at the cover of his book, as if he needed a reminder, and then told me a title by Edith Wharton. I don't remember which one, but he said he was writing an article about this book, comparing it with something by Henry James and focusing on modernism's relationship to realism, or something like that. I was concentrating on his jaunty little demeanor as he spoke, more than on the actual words he was using. He looked like a happy cherub as he babbled on, but then after a while he wound down, and his face returned to its plain roundness or round plainness.

"I suppose this sounds very dull to you," he said sheepishly. I noticed he was blushing.

"I guess I've heard duller things," I answered, in a tone that suggested that maybe I hadn't. When he laughed at that, it surprised me, not the least of all because I liked the sound of his laugh, a sort of joyful trilling I didn't expect.

"I'm Fisher," he said. "Fisher Dunleavy."

"Vincent Marshall," I said, pointing to my bare chest.

Later, when we went out for the first time, Fisher would tell me he was still in the grieving process. He'd lost his partner, Charles the Great, as I would come to think of him. When Fisher started to surface from that long hibernation (that day in the park), I was the one who happened to be there, with my clean-cut appearance and my wide, flawless grin, though my fresh-faced looks didn't exactly reflect my less-than-wholesome history. I suppose that was when the lies started and the omissions too. When he asked me about my past, I made up a sunny childhood in a pretty little town by a slow-moving river, conjuring the life of a teenage jock, complete with baseball championships, broken fingers during football games, and winning baskets at the buzzer. I was tall, strong, and athletic, so at least I looked the part. Then, for sympathy, I stirred in some bigoted parents (bullying father, devout mother) who tossed their boy from the house when he came out to them at eighteen, scattering his clothes and possessions on the lawn, like the aftermath of a boiler explosion.

I knew Fisher would question me about my higher education. He taught English at City College, so of course it was going to come up. I told him I'd attended a tiny liberal arts school in northern Maine. It was a place I knew about because someone from one of my temp jobs had gone there and made jokes about it, how it was basically a summer camp where you could get a degree. Fisher had never heard of the place. I was self-deprecating about this college and the education I fake-got there. So later on, if I missed one of Fisher's quasi-intellectual references or if my grammar failed me, I could blame it on my haphazard, backwoods schooling. I threw in some standard descriptions of evergreens, lobster dinners, and Maine accents to give the account the proper New England ambience and left it at that. This seemed to satisfy him. It was an education (I explained to Fisher) that had been paid for with high-interest loans and odd jobs. Of course, if it were happening today, I would do better research with the help of the internet. I'd scan Wikipedia pages for more interesting and varied details. I might lie about a better school. Or maybe, if I was meeting Fisher all over again, I wouldn't lie at all.

It was certainly easier to tell Fisher I'd gotten a spotty education on a bucolic Maine campus than to admit that I'd never applied to colleges at all. Getting my high school diploma had felt like the bittersweet end to a hostage crisis. I couldn't tell him what I'd really been up to for the four years after high school in Pennsylvania. There wasn't much of a positive spin I could have put on the depressed town where I grew up, or my half-dozen lost jobs in fast-food joints, or my succession of drug-dealing boyfriends. And it wouldn't have been a happy choice to bring up my own brief dependency on painkillers either, which had been a fucking bitch to kick. I'd been arrested a couple of times too, for trespassing and disorderly conduct, done some community service, and had my record expunged. At least I was able to recognize the dead-end quality of that life, its grim futility, like fishing line tightening around my neck.

When I got to New York City, I'd noticed there was plenty of futility here too, but it was gussied up like a drag queen, with dirty glamour and street noise. I found temp work, but two years later I was barely getting by. I lived in a small apartment in Alphabet City with two roommates. One guy danced nights in a cage at a leather bar in the Meatpacking District, and the other was a grad student in anthropology at NYU. Our building had the blown-apart look of collateral damage, and the walls of our apartment were grimy and pitted, like the complexion of a grubby teenager. There were cockroaches in our cereal every morning, and we had a neighbor who shot off M-80s in the middle of the night.

I preserved a few of the real details about my life—the temping and the crummy apartment—though I turned my cage-dancing roommate into a Canadian bartender. I told Fisher I was saving up so I could apply to law school, so I could one day work on treaties for some international environmental concern. I'm not sure where I came up with that one, but I revealed some volunteer work I hadn't really done for the Central Park Conservancy, though I had worn an orange vest for several months, picking up soda cans and used condoms from the side of the road in Pennsylvania, as part of my court-ordered community service.

I sanitized my sexual history for Fisher too, inventing a winsome roommate from the college I never went to, who wreaked havoc with my heart, and a lacrosse player I rolled around with a few times. I professed an aversion to casual encounters, telling Fisher I was basically this rather bashful sort of person, despite my hunky and robust appearance. I didn't mention my larcenous ex-boyfriends back home or my safari work with Buzz at the bars or the jerk-off video I'd done a few months earlier for some troll I met at an after-hours club because I was short on rent money.

It wasn't really so astonishing when I began to view Fisher as the potential antidote to my snakebit existence. I figured if I could create a sweet, winning image for myself, it would be better for everybody. From the beginning, Fisher wanted to see only the best in me anyway, like some indulgent grandmother in a storybook about naughty children. So I wove this earnest narrative into something modest and believable and, with the help of some bright smiles, a cheerful mood, and my habitual gee-whiz line readings, I became something to Fisher that I had never been with anyone else before: irresistible.

This was many years ago, back in the eighties.

We'd been out on a few dates before I finally agreed to go back to his place, thereby further demonstrating my innocent ways. Fisher lived in a two-bedroom co-op in a doorman building on Riverside Drive. He seemed both proud and nervous while showing me around for the first time. The entrance foyer of the apartment led into an oversized living room with several built-in bookcases, some sleek furniture, and a working fireplace. There was a formal dining room, which was rarely used, Fisher said, as if describing a disappointing relative he didn't like to visit. The wood floors throughout the apartment were rich and glossy. They shimmered like sheets of ice. The bedrooms were good-sized, the closets as deep as small caves. It was a prewar building, and Fisher pointed out the moldings and other original details with the glee of an archaeologist showing off the results of a successful dig. Coming from the combat zone that was my downtown apartment, I was duly impressed.

The master bathroom was really something special, with its art deco fittings and huge glassed-in shower sporting half a dozen showerheads. It could fit a rugby team, if one were so inclined, though I caught myself before making that particular observation. Best of all, off of this was a utility room with a washer and dryer. Outside of the city, these things—large closets, fireplaces, laundry rooms—were standard-issue, but in Manhattan they were prized above jewels.

It was a corner apartment on a high floor. Sun spilled through the windows at all times of day, and there were river views, Fisher told me, but now it was night, so all I could see of the outside was the black marble sky and the lights of New Jersey winking in the distance. Aside from all the books, the entire space was neat and streamlined, in the manner of an airplane hangar. But on most of the pale walls and on nearly every surface, even in the kitchen and bathrooms, there were framed photos of Charles.

Sometimes Fisher (a younger and better-looking version of him) was standing next to his late spouse in some kind of rollicking pose, but mostly these pictures featured Charles alone, square-jawed and dashing—rappelling down a rock wall, steering a kayak, deep-sea fishing. It was like paging through an L.L.Bean catalog with only one model. When Fisher told me, over dinner on our first date, that Charles had died at the age of forty-six, he had been quick to add, "It wasn't

AIDS," as if by assuming this it would somehow sully the memory of their ironclad monogamy.

"I didn't think that," I said defensively, though of course I had, given the realities of the world we were living in and my own cynicism about idyllically monogamous relationships.

Fisher had told me he met Charles at Dartmouth, tossing a Frisbee around on the quad, which seemed an appropriately sun-dappled beginning for these two. Not long after this, they'd fallen into each other's arms and embarked on the kind of iconic, against-all-odds gay romance that now spawns so many indie films.

"It was acute lymphoblastic leukemia," Fisher explained. "Charles was sick for a long time, and he held on a lot longer than anyone imagined he could. Even the hospice nurses, who'd seen everything, couldn't believe it. He's been gone almost three years now."

Fisher still seemed numb and hollowed out when he told me this. I offered up what I guessed were the right sympathetic sounds, but I didn't have much experience feeling sorry for anyone, so I wasn't sure how convincing I was. Now, on my first visit to the apartment, as we reentered the living room after our little tour, I picked up one of the photos from a bookcase: Charles in a Mets cap in front of Shea Stadium, smiling and carefree, like a guy in a beer commercial, the way he looked in all of these shots, more or less.

"Charles, huh?" I said.

"Yep, that's my husband," Fisher answered solemnly.

"Handsome," I said.

"Yes," Fisher said, as if he were confirming the existence of gravity.

Fisher always referred to Charles as "my husband" or "my spouse," though this was long before marriage equality . . . or cell phones, for that matter, or Facebook, or lots of other things we now take for granted.

I stood there with the photo of dead Charles in my hands, trying to behave as a kinder person might. Fisher took the photo from me and then we sat on the sofa together. I hoped he wasn't going to hug the frame to his chest or sit there ticking off a list of his spouse's virtues and assets. From previous conversations, I already knew that Charles had done well in real estate and later run a successful catering business before he took ill. It was his money that had purchased the apartment we were sitting in. And, after seeing all these photos, I also knew the guy was great-looking and adventurous. This seemed like more than enough info for one night.

"You see, the thing of it is," Fisher was saying to me now on the sofa, "I haven't had anyone here since Charles passed. Men, I mean. And, actually, there's never been anyone else for me other than Charles. So, you coming here is kind of this rather miraculous situation. I mean, it's a somewhat unprecedented event, actually. And you could say I am a bit flummoxed, because I happen to like you quite a bit, Vincent, and I am not sure what your opinions are of me or on the subject in general."

When he got nervous, Fisher spoke in a stilted and formal way, maybe because of all that Edith Wharton and Henry James he read. As he explained this about himself, there was that prim, embarrassed smile again too, the one from that day in the park. I found myself reaching out to touch Fisher's cheek. I told myself it was because I wanted him to stop talking, but before I knew it, I was taking the photo out of his hands, putting it carefully aside, and pulling him toward me.

✳

Fisher asked me to move in with him eight days later. I'd been on Riverside Drive less than a month when Buzz insisted on visiting. He made a hooting sound when he walked in the front door and then wandered about the place, singing "Movin' On Up," the theme song from *The Jeffersons* in a mincing falsetto.

I was glad Fisher was at his office hours at the college, which was how I'd planned it.

"It's *purdy* here," Buzz said after he stopped singing, "but a bit stark and anorexic, if you ask me. It's like the Karen Carpenter of apartments. I don't mind the white walls, but really, honey, where's all the stuff?"

I'd been to Buzz's studio apartment, which was cluttered with clothes, magazines, and empty fast-food containers. His place was brimming with chaos and unanswered questions, like a crime scene.

"Yeah, I guess we keep it pretty tidy," I told Buzz.

I didn't mention that there was a storage space in Chelsea with all the clothes and things that belonged to Charles, plus the accumulation of memorabilia from their lives together, everything Fisher couldn't bear to see every day but didn't want to get rid of either.

Buzz and I sat at the kitchen table, where he admired the fancy appliances. It was a nice, gleaming kitchen, the kind you see on television cooking shows. I had put a bowl of grapes out and poured us some water. I wasn't offering anything else. I didn't want Buzz to get too comfortable. Fisher's office hours weren't going to last forever.

He popped a grape in his mouth.

"So, it's really nice here and all," he said, "but wouldn't it be better if you could convince your guy to get you your own place? I mean, if

Dr. Feelgood was around twenty-four seven, I'd put a staple gun to my head in no time. I like my independence."

I didn't mention that sleeping with a sixty-year-old orthopedist to get your rent paid was a funny way to define independence.

"Well," I said, "it's not twenty-four seven, is it? I mean, Fisher teaches his summer classes, and he has office hours and faculty meetings and events at the school, and I'm working too."

"That's another thing," Buzz said. "Why are you still temping? You seem to be doing this all wrong. This was supposed to get you out of all that. Wasn't it?"

I shrugged. I didn't tell Buzz that I was probably never going to be the kind of hustler he wanted me to be. I was even contributing to the rent, though Fisher refused to take anything more than what I had been paying in Alphabet City.

"Look," Buzz went on, "if the good doctor wants me to dress only in blue and draw a face on my dick so he can play with it like a puppet, I'll gladly comply. But the flip side of that is, he pays my bills and I don't have to see him all the time. Lord knows he's clingy enough as it is, calling me up in the middle of the night to see if I'm home. And if I'm not, he gets all jealous and possessive, like some fourteen-year-old girl, though his threats still come out of him like the pudgy old man that he is."

I could hear a trace of Buzz's southern accent as he ranted, which he usually tried to hide. He was obviously from down south somewhere, though he'd never name a state or a town, preferring to keep his past concealed from view, as if it had slipped into some witness protection program. I imagined, though, that as Buzz aged, the accent would return, the way a past color bleeds to the surface of a weather-beaten house. I could also see this Buzz of the future avoiding harsh lighting, draping himself over daybeds, and trying to seduce paperboys, like Blanche DuBois.

"But perhaps in your case," he went on, "I've misread the whole situation, and what we have here is what is commonly referred to as a relationship."

"Don't be ridiculous," I said, surprised by the righteous indignation in my voice. "I only moved in because it's a hell of a lot better here than Avenue C. I'd be an idiot not to take advantage of that, as you should know better than anyone."

"Okay, okay," Buzz said, laughing and raising his hands up in mock surrender. Then he sipped some water and switched gears. "Well, how about the sex? How do you even fuck with good old Chuck staring down at you from every possible angle?"

Buzz had noticed all those photos of Charles right away as he was traipsing around the apartment, and I'd already given him a quick rundown.

"We manage," I said.

"So it's good, then?"

"What is?"

"The screwing. Don't be dense."

"Christ, Buzz. It is what it is."

"Oh my God. So touchy!"

"I'm not being touchy. But have you ever heard of the word *privacy*?"

"I don't know," Buzz said. "I think I have. Is it the same privacy you employed when discussing your wrestling weekend in the Hamptons? You covered every inch of that story without taking a fucking breath."

He was grinning like an imp.

"Don't be an asshole," I said.

I couldn't exactly say what I felt for Fisher at that particular moment, but I wasn't going to turn him into some horny, absent-minded-professor punch line for Buzz either. That's not how it was at all. Fisher wasn't some creeper. If anything, I think our age difference embarrassed him. I definitely couldn't tell Buzz how Fisher had actually wept the first time we messed around, how sometimes all we did since then was hold each other and kiss—though when we did have sex, it was always fun and suitably hot. What I wasn't prepared for was Fisher's tireless affection. He might rub my back for a full hour, making slow circles, kissing me between the shoulder blades as I stretched like a cat in the sun. I certainly enjoyed this attention more than the sweaty, heaving encounters I'd had with those old guys from the bar. Even my boyfriends in Pennsylvania, who were rarely sober or fully present when we went to bed, hadn't been up to much.

Meanwhile, I was learning other stuff too. On my nightstand was a stack of books, classics mostly, that Fisher had pulled for me from his bookcases. I didn't have a particularly curious mind, but I was slowly working my way through this stack. I sort of liked Fisher's makeshift attempts to improve my education. He'd also given me his own collection of literary criticism, which was called *A Place in the World,* essays written in his deliberate and straightforward voice, a discussion of gay subtext in the classics.

"My book," he had said bashfully as he handed it over, "such as it is."

Fisher showed me around the city too, taking me to museums and art films, a couple of concerts, the ballet once. We'd gone on walking tours of the Village and the Lower East Side, visited the Edgar Allan Poe Cottage in the Bronx. How Buzz would have howled if I had mentioned all this improvement and activity! I could just hear him calling me a West Side construction project, telling people I'd been closed for repairs. He would have moved on from *The Jeffersons* theme to singing me the entire score from *My Fair Lady*.

"Well, I certainly wouldn't want to invade your privacy, dearie," Buzz said now as we sat in the kitchen. "But let me ask you something. Do you happen to have anything else to eat in this lovely place other than these motherfucking grapes?"

I hadn't expected things to go well when Fisher introduced me to his friends either. I was certain they would view me with suspicion and hostility from the start, afraid anything I said would expose me as the twentysomething fraud that I was. Instead, the warmth and casual regard they cast upon me shocked me into silence.

Fisher's best friend, Vern, who was about his age and taught in the same department at the college, would watch me with an odd mixture of longing and dismay, but he was always polite. Though once, when Fisher had taken a phone call and we were left sitting alone in the living room, he said, "Fish has been through a lot, you know, but he seems quite happy again. Let's keep it that way, shall we?"

His tone was cordial enough when he said this, but his eyes were hooded and probing, as if he could see right through me, all the way back to Pennsylvania and straight into my heart.

"Yes" was all I could think to say. "Let's."

Fisher often talked me up like a press agent with Vern and his other friends—with Jim, who did something for the UN, and Jim's wife, Clare, a fundraiser for a dance troupe, and Noreen, who lived in Fisher's building and was a prop master for Broadway shows.

They were all established, successful, and middle-aged, these people. I realize now that Fisher must have looked pretty foolish as he bragged about my alleged high school athleticism, my phantom plans for law school, and my real-life temp work. Even my invented persona, the main ingredients of which were law-abiding modesty and youthful effervescence, didn't leave much to boast about. And still Fisher praised my wit and had me do my impressions of some of the lawyers I'd encountered at work, and this did get some genuine laughs. He was always trying to put me forward, to have me share my own opinions.

"So, Vincent, tell Clare what you thought about the Degas exhibit at MoMA," he might say, nodding and smiling.

At which point I would usually just mimic whatever he had said, but in a bubbly and interested tone. Maybe he was trying to prove to these people that I was somehow more worthy and substantial than I appeared. Maybe Fisher was trying to prove it to himself, especially after all those golden years with Charles.

It soon became clear to me, however, that the goodwill swimming my way from his friends had very little to do with any first impressions I had made but was instead the result of the love all these folks felt for Fisher. I was simply benefiting from my own proximity to him. It was like reflected sunlight or the clear skies brought on by a high-pressure system. Vern's devotion to Fisher was especially obvious in every heart-crushing glance he aimed in his old friend's direction. None of these people would have hurt him for the world, and so I was given a free pass and they left me alone.

I occasionally gave thought to coming clean, to just telling Fisher the truth about my past. I mean, was my actual history really all that bad? So, I never went to college. So, I'd been arrested a couple of times. So, I'd had a substance abuse problem, been to bed with some guys for cash and prizes, and shot a porn video. I hadn't killed anybody. But I figured I'd probably have to lead with that part and work my way backward. "Look, I never killed anybody, but . . ."

Fisher was the sweetest person I'd ever known. His sweetness fizzed up from deep within him like water from a secret spring or something, but he also had the sort of strict moral compass that prevented him from taking free soda refills at McDonald's. I was worried that my revelations might devastate him—and also get me kicked out into the street.

One night in bed, in the middle of the summer, while we were curled around each other, the ceiling fan whirring above us, Fisher told me about how hard it had been for him and for Charles when they first came out, after they'd fallen for each other and begun to share a life. This had been pre-Stonewall. Their families had disowned them immediately, which was crushing for both of them, though later there would be reconciliations and apologies. He was telling me this, Fisher said, because he was worried I must still be suffering from the estrangement with my own parents and from the memories of being physically tossed from my home.

"I just don't want you to give up hope about seeing them again," he said. "My people came around eventually, and that was over twenty years ago. It's a better world today."

Of course, the truth was that I had never come out to my parents at all and was long gone before they had the option of banishing me.

They didn't even live together, having gotten divorced when I was twelve, each marrying the person they had waiting in the wings and starting new and improved families. After that, I became superfluous, like an extra nipple or a sixth toe, as I bounced back and forth between the two busy, growing households. My teenage attitudes and trouble-making ways didn't exactly help matters. But I'd never been the center of attention anyway, even before the divorce. I suppose I was the living reminder of the bad blood that existed between my parents and the unhappy life they had previously shared.

By high school I was mostly on my own, couch surfing at friends' places most nights or occasionally shacking up with guys I'd met in the Harrisburg bars, which I would crash with a fake ID. I rarely saw my parents after I got out of school. I think that old phrase describes it best: there was no love lost between us. They knew I'd gone to New York, because I'd approached them both for some financial help with the move, which they had each categorically refused.

We hadn't been in touch since then, which was perfectly fine with me.

However, Fisher's concern had an impact on me that night. I knew he had really fallen for me. I should have told him the truth right then. He might have been as sympathetic to this real story of my family as to the one I had fabricated, and then who knows what might have happened? But that thought didn't occur to me until much later. Besides, I wouldn't have done anything to jeopardize the trip to Denmark.

In August, after the summer session ended at the college, Fisher was supposed to present his paper on modernism at a conference in Copenhagen, a city he had visited before and liked. I would go with him to Copenhagen, but first we would be meeting up with some friends of his, a straight couple he'd known for many years. They had rented a vacation house at the northern tip of Denmark, and we would be staying with them for a few days. It would be "our first little holiday together." That was how Fisher described it. I had never even been on a plane before, let alone out of the country. I chose not to lie about this, and Fisher found it rather charming. He paid to have my passport application expedited, bought the tickets, and made all the arrangements.

Buzz, of course, was ecstatic for me and probably a little jealous, an all-expenses-paid trip being the equivalent of hard currency.

"Finally," he said when I told him. "Some progress."

The notion of foreign travel had always appealed to me—the possibilities of glamour and fresh surroundings and the idea that one day I could tell people about the places I'd been, as if I was a citizen of the world. We flew from JFK into Copenhagen, on a plane filled with so many high-spirited summer backpackers that it felt like an airborne keg party.

We arrived in Copenhagen in the early morning, then changed planes and flew north to the Aalborg airport, where Fisher's friends were to pick us up. The winds were strong on the short flight, and our small plane was tossed around so violently that I was too frightened to look out the window. I was a big guy, used to swaggering around at all hours in rough neighborhoods. Nothing much scared me, so my discomfort amused Fisher some, though he patted my hand anyway and whispered some reassuring things in my ear.

We were picked up in Aalborg by his friends Nils and Freida, who, when they weren't on vacation like this, lived on a small farm in northern Sweden. Fisher told me he and Charles had been quite close to this couple, traveling with them on a number of occasions, all around Scandinavia and to other destinations in Europe. Fisher had met them during a sabbatical year when he was doing some research for a book on Isak Dinesen, a project he'd eventually abandoned. I was surprised when I first saw them waving at us across the terminal, this short, bespectacled pair in their mid-fifties. I suppose I was expecting some vigorous Nordic specimens or maybe actual Vikings. They hadn't seen Fisher since Charles died, as they'd been unable to come to the funeral, so there was a difficult moment at the airport when the three of them fell upon one another and hugged for a long time. Fisher's face looked watery and crumpled when he pulled away from this embrace, but the Swedes were more in control of their emotions and they just blinked a lot. They greeted me with brisk kindness and then we headed off in their poky little car for the trip to Skagen, where they had rented the house.

The flat, grassy countryside that streamed past didn't look too different from what I remembered of that ill-fated trip to the Hamptons with the banker, except here the houses were more modest and spread around the landscape like markers on a board game. Then we reached Skagen, and the scenery and the quality of light stunned me to the point of disorientation. The town was situated on a peninsula, against a wild landscape of shifting dunes, field grasses, and fir trees. The light was spellbinding, like flashbulbs going off everywhere I looked. The white-sand beach strobed and popped before my eyes, and the sky rose above the rolling ocean like a great blue screen. It was the place on the map where the Baltic meets the North Sea, their waves clashing for eternity.

As Nils drove (in an erratic and worrisome manner), Freida turned around from the front seat to point out some landmarks (the art museum, a lighthouse or two). She spoke slowly, in careful English. Her phrasing was genteel, and she had a hint of a British accent, making her sound like a governess in one of the old costume dramas that Fisher liked to rent at the video store.

The vacation house was close to the beach, yellow-plastered, with a red-tile roof and a white picket fence.

"A typical Skagen house," Nils told us as we climbed out of the car.

He spoke faster than his wife, but with the same formal lilt in his voice. Fisher and I were to have the large bedroom on the second floor, which was sparsely furnished, with just the bed and a pine dresser. The windows looked out to the impeccable beach and the sea beyond. We'd slept some on the plane, but after we put our bags down, Fisher and I stretched out on the bed, with its clean white sheets, to rest for a while.

"We've arrived," Fisher whispered as he reached out to hold my hand. He'd been watching me with a sort of shrugging wistfulness ever since we left New York, and it pleased me now to shut my eyes and focus on all the miles we'd traveled between here and there.

I liked the Swedes, their blunt observations and unfussy ways. They were friendly to me, treating me like a lost pet who had stumbled into their yard. I felt that at any moment they might pat me on the head. They smiled encouragingly whenever I joined in the conversation or asked questions. And I saw them notice the affection in Fisher's eyes when he glanced my way, and I could tell that this pleased them too. Our age difference didn't seem to faze them—perhaps evidence of Scandinavia's tolerance for free love, a stereotype I'd occasionally seen perpetuated on the silly American sitcoms of my childhood.

Fisher spoke enough Swedish for the three of them to fall into private conversations every once in a while, as we walked into town or picnicked on the beach. I wondered if this was when they spoke of Charles (I heard his name now and then in the gale of foreign words), perhaps sharing some memory of their time together on some longer, better vacation. I used to think that Charles couldn't be so perfect, that something dark and sinister would eventually surface about him, that he'd be revealed as an embezzler or a pyromaniac, a bully or a cheat. But aside from an apparent fondness for eating in bed and a habit of losing his keys (the only two examples Fisher offered when I pressed him for some less-than-flattering details), Charles continued to float around us pretty much as advertised, no matter which language was being spoken.

At supper on our third evening in Skagen, we were sitting around an old wooden table in the kitchen. Fisher had dubbed this furniture "Danish not so modern." We were eating some typical examples of the local cuisine: pickled herring and liver paste. There was a discussion going on about the differences between Sweden and the USA, a favorite topic of the Swedes, who seemed to admire the States, but in measured doses.

"Your America is such a brutal and sentimental country," Freida announced at one point, citing the dismal legacy of the Vietnam War and a Hollywood date movie they'd reluctantly seen.

"Yep," Fisher agreed, "that sounds about right."

"In Sweden this would not happen," Nils said, shaking his head, but I was unsure whether he was talking about Vietnam or the film or maybe both.

"This would not happen in Sweden" and "In Sweden this would not be allowed" were common retorts on the part of Nils and Freida. Earlier, they had explained that, in Sweden, baby names had to be approved by the government. You couldn't name your kids after rock bands or anything else that might seem whimsical. This didn't seem to bother them much. The rest of the conversation that evening had centered on our sightseeing experiences in the town and Fisher's upcoming conference in Copenhagen, which he was looking forward to. I stayed quiet, grinning good-naturedly at them. I realized that these grins, along with my cheerful reactions and easygoing demeanor, had become my trademark personality. I felt like an overaged Boy Scout, but this, after all, was the persona I had created for Fisher, the one he had fallen for and that had brought me here.

I continued to eat, wondering whether I preferred the liver paste to the gravad laks, the salt-cured salmon we'd had for lunch that afternoon. We'd picnicked on the beach with the salmon and some rye bread sandwiches, hunks of Havarti cheese, and bottled water. Something had happened at the picnic. I was still thinking about it. After I'd eaten my sandwich, I had wanted to go for a swim, but Fisher and Nils and Freida told me the water was much too cold for that, even though the day itself was sunny and warm.

"You'll regret it," they all said.

Their snooty disapproval annoyed me. I was, after all, a functioning adult. I noticed a group of young people a bit farther down the beach, wading in the waves, so I shucked off my T-shirt, threw it at Fisher, and headed their way.

The boisterous little group greeted me happily when I joined them in the water—which was freezing, as I'd been warned, but I was too stubborn to turn back. I made some obvious comments about the bone-chilling temperature, and everyone laughed. They might have been high or even a little drunk. It turned out they were Danish friends in their twenties, two men and three women, renting out another vacation house on the beach. It was tough to say how any of this crowd was paired up, but the most beautiful one of the group, muscular, blond, and male, took a liking to me immediately.

This guy tottered over as the waves crashed around our midsections and shook my hand. He squeezed my shoulder and asked in flawless English how long I had been in Skagen, where I was staying, and where I was from. He seemed very impressed that I lived in New York City, mentioning some Martin Scorsese movies and a magazine article he'd read about the Chelsea Hotel. From the moment he approached me, his intentions were unmistakable and breathtaking, spoken in the universal language of arousal and pursuit. His friends all seemed amused by this and even joked with him in Danish. They were probably used to his flirtatious, philandering style. The other guy there didn't seem to mind. He was just as amused as everybody else, so I assumed these two weren't a couple, but who knew what their situation was? This was Denmark.

"Are you traveling with your . . . parents?" the guy, whose name was Alfons, asked me as he motioned up the beach. He smirked when he asked this, as if he had already figured everything out concerning my past, present, and future. I looked back over my shoulder at the picnic. I could tell Fisher was watching us now, but I hoped he wouldn't yell anything or come my way.

"No, I'm here with my . . ." I could have said anything to this stranger. Instead, I just let the answer hang there, like the gulls circling above us. Then I dove into the water and took some strokes. I bobbed around about twenty yards from shore, catching my breath. Alfons had followed me out. For a while we treaded water, just staring at each other. He was so ridiculously handsome, I laughed out loud.

"I come out here every morning about five," he said. "There's no one on the beach at that time. You should come."

His smile was dazzling.

I was buzzed by the flattery, the unexpected lightning-quick aspect of it. Even in the icy water, I could feel myself getting hard.

"Thanks," I said, looking toward the beach, where Fisher had stood up and was kicking sand around, "but probably not this trip."

I swam back to shore.

At the dinner table that evening, Nils and Freida suddenly turned their attention to me, bringing me back from my vivid musings on Alfons. It felt as if someone had switched a light on over my head. Later I would wonder if I had misread their affection and they were instead conducting some sort of fact-finding mission.

"So, Vincent, where are you from in America exactly?" Nils asked.

"And what do you do?" Freida said at the same time. "Fisher says it is some kind of *momentary* work."

Laughing, I named the region of Pennsylvania I was from, describing it, as I'd done with Fisher, in conventional small-town terms, without mentioning the smokestacks, pervasive racism, or drug trade. Then I did my best to explain temping, though this was not a concept the Swedes appeared to understand.

"We do not have this in Sweden," Freida said with finality.

I laughed at that too and smiled some more. It was all very friendly and pleasant. And then Nils asked where I had gone to school, so I named the small college up in Maine.

"Oh, I know that place," Nils said brightly. "We spent a good deal of time in Maine one summer. It reminded us of our area of Sweden. Do you remember, Fisher? We flew over and stayed with you and Charles in Manhattan for a week and then Freida and I drove up to Maine and Canada for the rest of our vacation."

Fisher nodded and poured himself some Danish wine.

"In what town was your school?" Nils asked. "I am sure we passed through this place. Isn't there a large stone cathedral in the middle of your campus?"

I stammered. I knew nothing about cathedrals. I didn't even know the actual town. I never had known, only that it was way up north.

"It was way up north," I said.

"Yes," Freida said, "but the town?"

There was a lengthy, awkward pause as they all stared at me with their glasses raised, as if there was about to be a toast.

"Outside of Portland," I muttered. Portland was the only city I knew in Maine. Why I didn't just make up a fake place, I'll never know.

"But that can't be," Fisher said. "Portland isn't anywhere near the northern part of the state."

"Oh, you're right," I said quickly, pounding the table so hard that the plates rattled. "But I used to fly into Portland on my way up there and then take a bus the rest of the way."

Fisher put his wineglass down.

"You used to fly into Portland? But you told me you'd never been on a plane before this trip."

I was breathing funny now, and I knew my face must be turning red. Did the Swedes understand the significance of what was going on? I couldn't tell. I only knew that it was the first time I'd seen Fisher look at me with anything other than trust in his eyes.

"Yes. No," I said stupidly. "It's true. I hadn't been on a plane before. That's right. Did I say I took the plane to Portland? I meant train."

My voice was high-pitched and artificial, a lunatic's voice. I wasn't convincing anybody.

There was still no answer about the name of the college town either, and that question swirled dangerously around the table for a moment like radon. Then Nils was telling us about how he and Freida had been stopped at the Canadian border by overzealous customs officials who had confiscated their jars of blueberry jam. They'd been practically strip-searched. I laughed too loud at this story, and when I looked over at Fisher, I saw he'd gone back to swigging his wine.

He didn't say anything later when we went up to our room, and I certainly wasn't about to start a major conversation right then, right there, halfway around the world and with the Swedes downstairs. Instead, he was quiet and polite as we got ready for bed, a muffled version of who he already seemed to be. When we climbed under the sheets, I turned away.

"Vincent, Vincent, Vincent," Fisher said gloomily, but I didn't answer. I waited for him to say something else, but eventually he turned away too.

His voice had sounded slurry. Maybe the wine had knocked him out. At home he didn't drink much. I wondered whether, because of the alcohol, he hadn't really noticed the slipup about the college town, or my own flustered and guilty reaction to it. This was a foolish thought. Of course he had. I began to resent the fact that I was being made to fret about all this, that it was keeping me awake. It didn't help that this far north, there was about twenty hours of summer daylight, and we had no curtains on those ocean-facing windows, so I lay awake for hours, dozing off briefly before I was jolted back into consciousness. The small travel clock next to the bed read 4:45. I wondered if my body was responding to some internal alarm, my erotic subconscious nudging me awake at the promise of muscular Alfons stalking the beach. I got up as quietly as I could, threw on some shorts, and slipped out of the house.

It was gray outside. I felt as if I were moving through a black-and-white photograph as I made my way toward the water. I was thinking (if I was thinking at all) that some bone-crushing sex with Alfons, a beautiful boy my own age, would be just what I needed to bring me back to myself. It seemed important, in that moment, for this to occur. I hadn't been myself for a while. And in some irrational way, I was still trying to blame Fisher for what had happened the night before with the Swedes. Maybe fucking around would help with that too. But when I got to the beach, there was no sign of Alfons. I mostly felt good about that, because my head had begun to clear by then and I was having second thoughts. Relieved, I turned back toward the house.

That was when I saw him cutting across the sand toward me in the dim light.

"I'm glad you decided to come," Alfons said as he approached.

Then he grabbed me and kissed me hard on the mouth. He led me along the shore to an area where the dunes were partly shielded by some high grass, where he pulled me down with him, yanking my shorts off and stripping off his own. His hands and mouth were on me everywhere. He was even more beautiful than he had looked in the water, but I was fully awake now and it was all happening too fast. I could tell this was a colossal mistake, some point of no return. But I couldn't stop it. My body was responding, all on its own, while my mind remained distracted and uneasy. All I could do was try to mimic Alfons's movements, as if I were following dance steps. Alfons could sense my reluctance, and this really seemed to annoy him. He wasn't used to indifference. He mumbled what I assumed were some unkind words in Danish and then he roughly pushed my head down to his crotch. At one point I thought I heard something above us, but as I tried to shift away, he continued to hold me down and slapped me hard on the jaw. When he was finished, he got dressed without even looking at me and stomped off down the beach. I sat in the dunes and imagined what it would feel like to be the kind of person who might cry in this situation.

After a while, I put my shorts on. The sun was up now and the sky looked rinsed and clean. I was alone on the beach. When I got back to the house, the Swedes were still asleep, but I could hear Fisher banging around upstairs. I went up to our room and watched him from the doorway as he rushed back and forth.

"Fisher," I said.

He was packing my bags in a frenzied way, whirling and spinning like a planet. He wouldn't look at me at first or acknowledge my presence. Then, in a sharp, unrecognizable voice, he explained how he had followed me that morning and seen me in the dunes with Alfons. "I should have known," he repeated a few times bitterly as he clambered about. "Vern has been warning me since I met you, but I was too stubborn to even listen to him. Too stubborn and too vain, no doubt. A fool for love. That's what they call it. First the stupid lies last night, and now this! Christ! Fuck! Shit!"

Fisher drop-kicked my toiletry bag across the room. I'd never heard him curse before. For that matter, I'd never known him to express any anger at all. It was surreal and mesmerizing to watch, as if his rage were some rare astronomical event. When he spoke, it sounded as if he wasn't getting enough air into his lungs. I remember thinking that someone needed to remind him to breathe. But I was having my own difficulties. I felt, in those moments, as if I might separate and rise up from my body, like the times when I went to bed with those guys from the bar—my old disappearing act.

"You must go now," Fisher said, his voice choppy, putting periods after each word.

Not only that, but I must never make any attempt to see him again. I could tell he meant what he was saying and that it would remain a nonnegotiable point. His voice was still breathless, but now he was over-enunciating everything, as if he were reading from cue cards at a high altitude. He had stopped pacing and begun to calm down. He handed me my plane ticket and my passport and a generous amount of cash, a mixture of Danish kroner and dollars. Although taking the bills, under those circumstances, humbled me, I didn't refuse them or give any back. (I didn't like to remember that part later.) Fisher told me to find my own way to Copenhagen, change my ticket, and leave the country as soon as possible. He would be staying for the conference, and he did not want us on the same flight back to New York. When he got home, he said, he would pack up my things and leave them with the doorman. Finally, he made me turn over my keys to the apartment, the expression on his face as wrecked and miserable as it had been the day the Swedes met us at the airport, when they'd all hugged one another, remembering poor, dead Charles. By then I knew we were beyond apologies or explanations. Those images from the beach were probably playing in his brain now on some lurid, continuous loop. I didn't try to say anything. I was in my own dazed state. I didn't say anything at all.

I didn't go back to New York City, not right away, at least. I had the money Fisher had handed over and more of my own, some extra cash hidden in one of my bags, which I realize, in retrospect, I might have put there in anticipation of some calamity. I also had a nice, expensive camera, a present from Fisher in honor of my first trip abroad, which I sold to a noisy Australian backpacker who admired it at the Skagen train station, which was where I had walked after I left the house. The minute he expressed his interest, I told him to make me an offer.

After that, I traveled around Europe, on the cheap, sleeping on night trains or checking into bustling youth hostels. I had made my way out of Scandinavia, first stopping in Amsterdam and then Brussels before I arrived in Paris. I stayed there for a while, gawking at the must-see attractions and wandering through the Marais, the city's gay district. I'd picked up some Let's Go guides at an English-language bookstore across from the Pompidou Center, which looked like a jumble of colored drainpipes. Then I traveled through the Alsace region, where it was cold and rainy most of the time. After that, I found myself in Lausanne, on the shores of Lake Geneva. This must have been very beautiful, but I mostly remember an art museum there, much touted, that housed the works of the mentally ill and the criminally insane.

I liked the aimless pace of all this, my loose adherence to time, my traveler's ingenuity. I was a leaf caught in a slow, foreign current. At the end of September, I found myself in Florence, of all places, and there, on my very first night, I met a married Italian in a bar. It was an establishment not so different from the ones I had frequented back in New York. He was an older man, of course, stocky and leering. He was a local wine merchant, it turned out, with an unhappy wife in Fiesole and a grown daughter in Milan. The daughter kept track of costumes for the glossiest productions at La Scala. Luca thought I was very handsome, or so he said in his passable, booming English. He pretended I was more amusing than I was too, nodding cheerfully at me whenever I spoke, working harder than was really necessary.

When I told him that I was just passing through and my funds were running low, he rented me a tiny furnished apartment on the fifth floor of a run-down building near Santa Croce, with a broken elevator and a crumbling marble staircase. He gave me a small allowance each week. In this way, I briefly became the Florentine version of Buzz, whom I'd been sending stupid and cryptic postcards from my various stops along the way. Most days I was quite idle, waiting for this man, who was not a particularly pleasant or intelligent person, to show up for some insistent, slobbering sex and a few shards of dull conversation. My Italian never got beyond the peppy salutations phase. I was aimless in Florence. I liked to visit the Uffizi (when there weren't strikes) and stand in front of the masterpieces, affecting a look of understanding and refinement, but the paintings didn't really transport me, not in the way the guidebooks told me they should.

One day, while standing in the Renaissance room, I heard an American woman say to her husband, "If I see one more John the Baptist Head on a Platter, I'll slit *my own* throat."

It had been a long time since I'd had a good laugh.

Every morning, I'd walk along the filthy Arno or hike up to San Miniato al Monte, the famous Romanesque basilica that sits at one of the highest points in the city. I'd stand in the plaza there, staring out at the famous view of Florence's terra-cotta roofs, and wonder about the mess I'd made. I couldn't stop thinking of Fisher. I wondered if I should have handled things differently after he confronted me with what he'd seen on the beach, if I should have confessed everything and told him how I felt about him and about our lives since we'd met. I probably should have done this, even if he refused to believe me. For the truth was, as I sat in those dunes rubbing my sore jaw, my feelings for Fisher had suddenly become quite clear. How anxious I was to see him that morning, on my way back to the house, as I crossed the sand!

When Luca tired of me (I'd become the grumpiest of rent boys) and the existence I was leading in Europe became unsustainable, I returned to New York, which was in the middle of another lousy winter. Buzz let me crash with him in his studio as long as I made myself scarce when the orthopedist showed up for their conjugal visits. It took me a while to pull it together, longer than it should have, but things could have turned out a lot worse. I did stop hustling eventually—my version of it, at least. In my thirties, I even went back to school part time and got a business degree. I was an office manager in a law firm by then, which has more or less become my career. My own time in the word-processing pool has made me sympathetic to the secretaries and temps, so most of them like me and don't give me any trouble. And I never let sentiment get in the way of staffing decisions either, and this is what the partners value most.

I came across Fisher's obituary today when I Googled him out of curiosity, something I'd never done before. He died last year, "after a brief illness." Since we parted ways in Denmark, he had written a few more books and retired from teaching. A devoted husband and step-children were listed as survivors, and a grandchild too. Charles the Great was also in there, of course, mentioned as the predeceased spouse. What pleased me was that he had apparently found love again in his life.

After reading about Fisher's passing, the memories of our time together came back to me suddenly and with some force, like a cloudburst—especially the ones from when we first met in the park. When my lunch hour ended that day, I had put my shirt on and stood up. Fisher had stood up too, rather hastily. He hadn't yet worked up the courage to ask if he could see me again. Something was telling me I should just leave this guy alone. As we were making our way out of the park, Fisher was carrying his blanket and towels and the work he'd brought with him. His books and papers kept spilling out all over. He looked like someone on a stage trying to get a cheap laugh. But finally, he got control of his belongings and looked up at me, flushed and hopeless, and that was when I first smiled at him, a true and proper smile, and I remember it came to me quite involuntarily, in spite of myself.

IF YOU ONLY KNEW

Before my father runs off, he suddenly showers us all with attention. It's jarring at first, like having someone crowd next to you on a bus when there are plenty of seats in back. There's something desperate about it, but I'm not thinking this at the time. I'm just thrilled to be part of his world, because up until then, he has been a shadowy figure, a supporting player in our lives. He's a busy executive, a senior vice president at a famous insurance company in Boston, coming home late most nights from work after my brother and I are in bed. I wait up for him, for his late-night, one-minute check-ins, first to Wylie's room across the hall and then to mine. He stands at the foot of my bed as he loosens his tie, squeezes my big toe.

"You awake, Sport?" he says.

I always make sure to keep my toes peeking out from under the covers so he can grab one, but because of pride or stubbornness I never say a word before he walks away.

He goes to the office most weekends as well, and when he doesn't, he leaves the house at dawn to play golf, which he tells us is work-related too. For business contacts. He calls golf a necessary evil, as if he's talking about a flu shot in the ass.

It is 1975.

He calls my mother every afternoon, usually to say he'll be taking the last train out of the city to our little suburb.

"Why does he do that?" I ask her once, after she puts the phone back on its hook. We are standing in the kitchen, the afternoon sun coursing through the windows, spilling over the Formica countertops. "Like he's telling you something you don't already know."

I have just turned thirteen and am getting a mouth on me.

"He likes to keep me informed," Ma says.

There might be an edge to her voice when my mother tells me this, or I might be remembering it that way, adding it in after the fact, like a sound effects engineer.

"Anyway," I tell her, "you should suggest he save his calls for some really big news, like when he's planning to make it home in time for a meal with his family."

"Now, Kevin," she sighs, "don't be so dramatic."

I already have a reputation.

"Ma!" I shout. "He's never here! Wiley pointed to the weatherman on Channel Four the other day and asked if *he* was our father!"

My little brother, of course, has never said such a thing; because he's ten years old and knows better, but I still see the impact of my wise-ass words flash across Ma's face like brush fire. Soon after this, it is summer, and they are remodeling my dad's offices and he is suddenly home full time, and this is when the attention starts. He lavishes himself on us. When it happens, I am willing to forgive everything that has come before. I am powerless against it anyway. It's like a natural disaster. He's my dad.

He takes Wiley and me to Fenway three times during those weeks to watch the Red Sox play. We win every time. At least my memory has it that way. My dad gets chummy with the guys selling concessions at the park, introduces himself to everybody sitting in our section, and makes up nicknames for total strangers. He slaps people on the back too, as if he's running for political office, but like with real candidates, this routine seems to divide the crowd. He makes an impression, all right, but I notice a few folks turn away and shrink back as if from an exposed power line. My brother is crazy out of his mind for Fred Lynn that summer, the rookie center fielder for the Sox who is having a phenomenal season. Every time the big guy comes up to the plate or lopes out to his position, Wiley stands up, waves his arms like a castaway, and yells "Frreedddie" in his shrill little voice. I am at the age when I get embarrassed by anything that causes strangers to look in my direction. I smack Wiley with my baseball glove and tell him to shut up. We always bring our gloves to snag foul balls, but they never come anywhere near us.

"Ease up on your brother, Sport," Dad says, and softly cuffs my ear. It is tough to be angry at Wiley. He is a sweet-natured, cheerful kid, and we rarely fight, which even then I realize is beyond miraculous for brothers. We love all the usual things about Fenway, the hot dogs, the hum of excitement, the quirky beauty of the place. Some years later, when I am flying over Ireland on my first trip abroad, I finally see colors that can compete with my lush green memory of that painstakingly maintained playing field. In Dublin I buy a postcard with a standard aerial shot and send it off to Wiley at Bucknell, scribbling *Frreedddie!!!!* on the back. I know he'll understand. We're brothers. We have joint custody over certain memories, visitation rights.

My mother doesn't come to the games, but she loves to hear us talk about them when we get home. Wiley spins with excitement, almost frothing at the mouth with it. He can remember every play, every moment, and he acts it all out like a stage production. And Ma says "oohhh" and "ahhh" in all the right places, like she's been waiting her whole life to hear such stories. Dad and I hang back a bit, off to the side, his arm draped across my shoulders, while we watch the show with big, wide grins on our faces.

We do a lot of things together as a family that summer. It's just ordinary stuff, but it's more than we've ever done before. We go to the Stoneham zoo and the aquarium at Central Wharf in Boston and a Mel Brooks movie that my mother worries about being too adult for Wiley and me.

"Lighten up, Gwen," Dad tells her in the refreshment line as she gawks nervously at Teri Garr's cleavage prominently featured in the lobby poster. He gives Ma a friendly hug. Then he looks over her shoulder, catches my eye, and winks, like we are sailors on shore leave.

We drive up to a beach on the North Shore during the week, when it isn't so crowded. Dad does a perfect backflip on the sand, teaches us how to bodysurf. The ocean is freezing, and Ma forces us to get out when our lips turn a phosphorescent blue. On our way home, we are sunburnt and gritty with sand, our hair stiff with salt. An announcer on the car radio mentions the first rendezvous in space between the Apollo and Soyuz spacecrafts, a hopeful sign for US and Soviet relations, and it adds to the optimism of the day.

At home that summer, after dinner, which we once again are sharing as a family, my father can't sit still. He moves and moves around the living room, telling jokes, doing his card tricks.

"Pick a card, any card, any card at all," he bellows, fanning the deck out in front of us like some Vegas hustler.

The tricks are lame, and I begin to figure them out, but Wiley ogles my dad as if he's a celebrity. And sometimes I can't help myself—so do I. My father was a jock in high school and college, and he still has an athlete's muscular grace. He is handsome and confident, but it goes beyond his good looks, his golf tan and perfect teeth. He is a hotshot businessman who is used to working a room. We are, I suppose, not unlike the people who report to him, a captive audience. Even that night I am aware he is performing. He wants something from us. Perhaps it is simple adoration, but much later the possibility will occur to me that we aren't in his thoughts at all.

My mother watches him too. She looks pretty and young in a pink sundress, wavy blond hair falling across her eyes. She has always been quiet, and her movements are often slow and deliberate, like she is trying to coax small animals out of the woods. Like Wiley and me, she seems to be enjoying herself, as if she is giddy with good fortune. Though I wonder now if she was also onto my father in some way, but helpless in the face of his summer onslaught just like me.

The remodeling of my father's office is completed, and he goes back to work. We slip quietly into the old patterns, but the summer memories are fresh and real, and they linger. We're still happy for a time. It is late August when I come downstairs and find my mother sitting at the kitchen table. She rarely sits around in the morning, so this is already suspicious. Usually she is preparing breakfast, putting it out for us, clearing it up. On this morning, though, she is dressed, but something isn't quite right about her. I think for a moment she is sick, but that would be truly unheard of. The dress she is wearing buttons up the front, but the buttons and holes aren't lined up right. I can see tiny ribbons of pink flesh through the material, the white of her bra. I am humiliated for both of us.

"Ma," I say, trying to avert my eyes, "your buttons are all messed up."

That's when she tells me that my dad has walked out. Her voice is flat and shocking, not like her own, or anyone's.

"Your father is gone," she says.

I know right away she doesn't mean he has simply left for work, but I ask her anyway if that is what she means. She sits up very straight.

"He has a new job," she tells me, "a sort of promotion, a transfer to California. I didn't know until he started packing last night. He took all his clothes except the winter things. I have no other way to say it, Kevin, so I am just telling you. He's not coming back. It's not about you or Wiley, obviously nothing you could have done. He needed to leave and that's where we are."

She has rehearsed this in some manner, I think. It sounds fake, practiced, like a bad script. Or something Dear Abby might advise—what to tell your kids when your husband suddenly bails on you. She must have been saying it for hours, over and over in her head, while waiting for me to come downstairs, and this is the terrible way it came out. It is totally ridiculous.

I make her say it again.

I ask if they had a fight, and she says no. She says he told her after Wiley and I had gone to bed, after his nightly check-in. I try to think if he waited at my door or held my toe a little longer, but I can't remember. I might even have been asleep. After the summer we just had, I felt bloated with attention, almost sloppy with it. There had been no need for me to wait up for him anymore.

"Didn't you tell him to stay?"

"I suppose I did," my mother says carefully. She has slumped back down in the chair now, like the air has been let out of her.

"You suppose? Why didn't you kick and scream and make him?" I ask.

I'd seen plenty of TV dramas by this point, and that's what jilted women usually did, but that wasn't Ma's style. A year before this, she ran up and down our neighborhood cheering and waving an American flag when Nixon resigned, but that was a rare display of emotion. Usually, she's unflappable.

"Kevin, he's been plotting it, okay?" she is saying. "The company has rented him an apartment out there already. He has a brand-new address. It's happening. He's on the plane right now. It's final."

She says this as if she can't quite believe it herself. I notice we are both shaking. I can hear the wall clock ticking off seconds above our heads, a reminder that our lives are moving on without us.

"Does he want to marry someone else?" I ask her.

In those same television movies, men were always deserting families for other women.

"He wouldn't say," she tells me, but averts my eyes.

I take that as a yes.

I can hear Wiley pounding around upstairs.

That's when she slips me a plain, sealed envelope. I honestly don't remember what my father had written. I know it seemed as phony as what my mother had told me, something about being a man, how I'd always be his son or some other foolish crap he scribbled down on his way to the door. What I do remember is the twenty-dollar bill that floats to the floor when I open the envelope. I let it land there. I don't pick it up. When I finish reading, I hand the note back to my mother without comment. I think she expects me to tear it up into tiny pieces or toss it down the garbage disposal, ever the little scene-stealer, but it is totally worthless as it is. She stares at me and her eyes begin to well up. She is sorry for me. I can see that, and that is when I feel my own tears coming, unstoppable as a seizure.

My mother has never even written a check before my father leaves for California. She has to get books about household finance out of the library. She takes it all very seriously and begins to get organized. About a week after my father leaves, she gets a small blackboard and writes out assignments and duties for all of us.

"We never had to help with laundry before," I whine, scanning the list of chores under my name. "Neither did Dad. You're passing off your own work."

"I have other things to worry about now," she says. "I need your help and your brother's. We have to be like a team."

"Sure, coach," I say, snapping my heels and giving her a salute.

Wiley is looking up at us both with a worried expression on his face.

"I'll help," he chirps.

"Pussy," I mumble at him.

My mother slaps me hard behind the ear, an unimaginable occurrence until that moment.

The three of us stand there stunned, unrecognizable, like visitors from another country, unsure of the official language.

"Do we understand each other?" my mother finally asks.

"Not really," I tell her, but she doesn't hit me again.

It's true my father leaves for that promotion my mother mentioned. But I'm right too. There is a woman named Delores Cantwell, a junior executive at his company who is being transferred to California at the same time. She has blown up her own marriage to be with my dad, but it's not as gross on her end because she doesn't have any kids to ditch. Perhaps she was one of his weekend golfing buddies. I never meet this woman. A few months after my father and Delores arrive in San Diego, feeling, as one can imagine, optimistic about their future, he is investigated for some financial and ethical improprieties. It's not quite embezzlement and the company does not press any charges, but my father is fired and finished in the insurance industry. Delores dumps him soon after. But instead of crawling back to us, my father stays in California to *explore his options*. He's a man who believes in making his own luck. I don't know all this at the time, but the essentials are pieced together later, as I get older, like the clues in a mystery novel.

We have the house, a three-bedroom Cape, in a modest neighborhood. My mother always refers to this as a mixed blessing. For years my father had been saying we'd move to a bigger place, in a more exclusive town, something more fitting with his growing importance at the company. He was only waiting for the right moment, but then he takes off for California before it ever comes about.

The house has a number of problems: a leaky roof, air in the pipes, a crumbling foundation. It groans at night like someone in the terminal ward. My mother checks out more books—*How to Be Your Own Electrician, How to Be Your Own Plumber*. We all get pretty handy, in a general way. We can recognize all the tools and tackle the minor repairs ourselves. For the longest time, Ma whispers "I can do this, I can do this" over and over, like it's her personal mantra, even if she is only changing a light bulb. And sometimes she mutters it as we pass in the hallway or sit at dinner, when there are no repairs in sight.

When my father loses his job in California, his checks stop coming, so my mother goes to work as a secretary at a law firm and takes classes part time so she can become a teacher. That's when she is pleased we don't have such a fancy house. She'd never be able to handle higher mortgage payments on her own. I am worried about her becoming a teacher. I am in junior high now, and teachers are known to have nervous breakdowns right in front of a class. Once, in physical science, we are passing a *Playboy* around under our desks when a substitute, a tiny, disheveled woman named Mrs. Hand, discovers it and starts calling us a bunch of "dirty little bastards." She is screaming like the building is on fire, waving her arms about. The assistant principal finally has to come and drag her away. The last thing she says before she is led out the door (the magazine rolled up tight like a baton in her fist) is that she is planning to pray for us, for our immortal souls. Needless to say, we never see her again. But for months afterward, my friends and I greet each other in the hallways with hoots of "How's it going, ya dirty little bastard?" while making the sign of the cross.

"You're not going to work at my school, are you, Ma?" I ask one night when she gets home from class. It is my night to cook dinner, macaroni and cheese. Wiley is setting the table. He has his own system. He doesn't like anything to match. The plates and glasses are an assortment of sizes, the silverware is from two separate patterns, and each napkin is a different color. Since Dad left, my mother doesn't care about this stuff, so long as we eat.

"Don't sound so terrified, Kevin," she says.

"I'm not terrified. I was only wondering."

"Well, beggars can't be choosers."

"What does that mean?"

"It means I need to work."

"But, Ma," I say.

"For Christ's sake, Kevin, if I get a job at your school, I'll take an assumed name and wear a goddamned veil over my head. Okay?"

"You never used to swear."

"It's a new day," she tells me.

A year or so after my father leaves us, my mother is still busy constructing our new life, and it is clear we are all going to survive, but that doesn't mean I am prepared for the next development. I come home from soccer practice one Saturday afternoon in September and find Oliver Voolich, the deli man from the First National, sitting on our sofa in the living room. It is a surreal moment for me, Voolich next to my mother, his hair slicked back, dressed in ill-fitting jeans and a plaid shirt. I am used to seeing him at the grocery store, paper hat perched on his head, greasy apron cinched at his waist, shouting out numbers for the next customer in line.

"Kevin, you know Mr. Voolich," my mother says, nodding in his direction.

"Yeah?" I grumble, but it comes out more like a question.

"You can call me Oliver," Voolich tells me.

"Hello, Mr. Voolich," I say.

"Oliver has been kind enough to offer to help us put up the storm windows this year," Ma says.

Voolich appears to be blushing furiously, or perhaps his skin just looks blotchier out from behind the deli counter. He has the round, pinkish face and squinty eyes of a newborn. There is definitely something soft and infantile about the whole package, even though I place his age at forty-five or so. He is of average height, though slightly stooped, with wide hips, a mess of curly brown hair and no discernible chin. When I later find out he lives in a single room above Shoe Town, this feels just about right and completes the picture.

At the deli counter, Voolich is patient and composed, good with difficult customers, scrupulously honest while administering the meat scale. But out here in the real world, hanging out in my living room, he is simply dull as rocks, so dull it hovers over him like body odor.

"We put up the windows by ourselves last year," I remind my mother, making sure not to make eye contact with our visitor.

"And we almost lost our lives in the process," Ma responds.

She has a point. The previous fall I had balanced precariously on top of the ladder while Ma hoisted windows up to me on the second floor.

Wiley had steadied the ladder directly beneath us. We were like mountain climbers tied to one another. We knew we were in harm's way.

It's obvious that Voolich wants to be of assistance, but naturally I question his intentions. We don't need anyone new in our lives. The truth is we are doing okay. The three of us have found a certain groove of living together. If I consciously miss my father, it is in the evening, when I remember his nightly check-in at the foot of my bed. Unlike most children of divorce, I hold no illusions about my parents reconciling. Although, since Wiley and I now are somewhat aware of Dad's financial scandal and the break with Delores, we half expect him to show up one day on the doorstep, shamefaced and eager to be forgiven, like a runaway pet. This never happens either. He barely keeps in touch with Wiley and me, while he's on his own twisted journey. Gifts arrive late, three months after our birthdays or Christmas. We suffer through phone calls laced with awkward silences. We get goofy, bizarre postcards from the guy. *If you only knew how much I miss you,* my father writes.

In the end, Voolich helps us with the windows, but the gawky sight of him on a ladder, drenched in sweat, laboring mercilessly, puts no one at ease.

"Good work, Oliver," my mother shouts up to him in an encouraging, anxious way as he finishes fastening the last one.

"Yeah, it's poetry in motion," I say quietly to Wiley, who gives me a look like he doesn't want me to start anything.

After this, Voolich apparently feels confident enough to insinuate himself into our lives a couple of times a week, often arriving with a smoked ham or a cold cut platter. He is a deli man. If he were a carpet salesman, he might come bearing throw rugs and vacuum cleaner bags.

Of course, by showing up with food, he can always count on an invitation to dinner, a fact he must have figured out for himself. My mother is always polite to him, but I notice she makes no other concession to his presence. When he joins us, she doesn't put on lipstick or tell Wiley the table settings need to match. Still, I can't be more disturbed than if she were sitting on his lap and sticking a tongue in his ear. To my way of thinking, she is treating him far too casually, the way she does Wiley and me, her own family, the fixtures in her life. And I hate the notion of Voolich becoming a fixture in *my life*. To my now fourteen-year-old brain, his florid face and sagging body represent failure and despair. I am worried about what my friends will say if they see him out with Ma. I can already hear a litany of "hide the salami" jokes.

Though my mother is the main attraction for Voolich, he often makes uneasy attempts to engage Wiley and me in conversation. He tells the same stories over and over again, droning accounts of his day behind a deli counter, with one day not any different from the last.

Once again it is Wiley who handles these situations gracefully. He politely answers idiotic questions concerning homework or sports, two more subjects Voolich feels compelled to discuss. However, I don't think the man is ever comfortable around us. He regards us, perhaps the way he views all children, with caution, as if looking over his shoulder in a rough neighborhood. This is brand-new territory for him. Privately, even my supersweet brother admits to his own reservations.

"Yep, he *is* a bit of a freakazoid," Wiley tells me on our way to school one morning.

"Exactly," I say.

"But that doesn't seem to bother Ma," he adds quickly.

"No," I say. "It sure as shit doesn't."

Voolich has been coming around for over a month when I decide it is finally time to confront her about the situation. I approach Ma late one evening as she is seated at the kitchen table, coursework spread out in front of her. It's her favorite spot for studying. Books and pencils are spilling everywhere. I notice she is wearing her hair longer, wilder, less like a housewife's and more like a student's.

"What can I do for you?" she asks without looking up from the notebook she is scribbling in.

"How long is this going to go on?" I ask.

"What are you talking about, Kevin?"

"You know what I mean. Voolich. Meat and cheese man. Is he going to become a regular thing around here?"

She looks up at me then, and I can tell she is slightly amused, giving me a prim, tired smile. She has hours of study ahead of her, the house to pick up, a new day looming tomorrow.

"He's a nice man," she says predictably.

"He bores Wiley and me under the table." I don't mind enlisting my brother in this campaign.

"Really?"

"Don't you think he's boring?"

"Kevin, I've heard enough sparkling conversation to last me a lifetime," she says.

And when she says this, I know she is referring to my father.

"Look," she goes on, "I don't really expect you to understand, but Oliver listens to me. He truly listens to me when I talk about my day, my time at school. This is a pleasure, and something I haven't really experienced before with another grown-up. It has never been easy for me to meet new people. I enjoy his company."

"Maybe it only seems like he's listening, because he's too tongue-tied around you to form actual words in the English language."

She doesn't respond to that, so I keep at it.

"Do you love this guy or something? Are you going to marry him?" I am horrified as I even say these things.

"Don't be ridiculous, Kevin." Ma laughs. "He's a friend. It's a harmless situation."

"Is he in love with you?"

"No," she answers cautiously. "Of course not."

I can tell she is weighing my question, maybe afraid to really look at it, like a puncture wound. I pause for a moment, the way a television anchorman switches gears before delivering the really serious news.

"Well, I just wanted you to know your sons are unhappy about this."

"Point taken," she says, but in such a way as to make it clear she has no intention of doing anything about it.

A couple of weeks after this, she comes into the living room, where Wiley and I are watching an episode of *Baretta*. She announces that Voolich has phoned and wants us to join him for an outing the following weekend.

"He wants to take us all to an amusement park, to Treasure Island," Ma says. "What do you think?"

We haven't done much in the way of amusement since my dad left town. Our finances and my mother's schedule don't warrant it. The term *entertainment expense* has not found its way into our weekly budget. So, despite my feelings for Voolich, my anxiety over his future role in our family, I can't help but look forward to the getaway he is offering us.

"Better than a wiener factory," I sigh, and even Wiley can't help but laugh.

When the day arrives, though, our adventure doesn't start out well. Voolich shows up earlier than expected and loiters around the kitchen as we finish our breakfast. He follows us from room to room, bites his lip, jangles the car keys in his trousers as we grab our jackets and put on our shoes.

"Are we in a hurry, Oliver?" my mother asks him.

"No, no, no. Take your time," he says in the sort of clipped, nervous tone that only gets us to move faster.

Voolich is so impatient to get on the road; I make sure to buckle my seat belt as soon as I settle myself in his car, a worn-out Plymouth. I think he might want to make up for lost time and risk our lives in the process. But once behind the wheel, he reverts to type, and we inch our way to the park, practically traveling in the breakdown lane. Treasure Island is located on the South Shore, halfway to the Cape. We pass a number of signs for the place on the trip down, advertising waterslides and a roller coaster. And on each colorful billboard, the park's official mascot, a pirate with an eye patch and a hook for a hand is featured, slyly beckoning to us.

Wiley is excited, bouncing lightly up and down in the seat beside me.

"Do you have to shit or something?" I ask him. But I am smiling when I say it, because I am excited too.

Then we get there.

Treasure Island is not even an island. It sits swelling like a festering blemish at the edge of a faded resort town. It's basically a huge parking lot, with some worn tents and kiddie rides strewn about, all enclosed by a rusty chain-link fence. There are about two dozen unsmiling people, grim employees and unsatisfied patrons alike, milling about under the bleak October sky, which has grown more overcast from the moment we pile out of the car. While Voolich goes to the gate to purchase the tickets, I glare at my mother with my arms folded across my chest. She's enjoyed herself on the trip down, chatting easily in the front seat with Voolich about her upcoming midterms, happy to be taking a break and to get out of the house. But now faced with her sons' disappointment, I can see she is concerned.

"I don't know what to say," she tells us, gazing around at our depressing surroundings. "But we're here now. We'll have to make the best of it."

"Okay," Wiley says.

"Dumbass!" I snap at him. "There's nothing for us here."

I get tired of my brother's perfect-little-man routine sometimes.

Voolich comes sauntering back, oblivious as hell until he takes one look at us and asks what the matter is.

"Treasure Island isn't exactly what the kids expected," my mother says diplomatically. "Not quite what was advertised on all those billboards."

"It's off-season, Gwen," Voolich tells her, as if this explains anything.

"You have to admit, Oliver, that it looks like the place has fallen on some hard times."

"More like hard times have fallen on *it*!" I say.

"I used to come here as a child," Voolich says, taking a long look around him, blinking at his own precious memories. "I suppose it *has* gone downhill, though."

"And there's no roller coaster," Wiley actually volunteers.

"I asked the fella at the ticket counter about that. Apparently there was an accident a few years ago, and they had to tear it down."

We all stand there for a while contemplating mayhem and disaster.

"Well, we don't have to stay," Voolich says in a quiet, defeated tone. I am ready to turn back toward the car, but he continues, "Or we *could* stay and give it a try."

"That's exactly what I told the boys," Ma says brightly.

The three of them turn and stare at me, waiting for my reaction, but since I don't really have a vote, I just roll my eyes and storm past them toward the entrance. Voolich clamors in front of me, back in his anxious mode. He leads us to the basketball toss and the roulette wheel, other games of chance, talking the place up like a press agent.

"Look at the prizes! There are some fine prizes to be had! Step right up, Wiley! It's on me! Go for it, pal!" Voolich gushes, rubbing the top of my brother's crew cut.

There is a ride called the Scrambler, the only one that isn't too infantile for us. Voolich has us ride it three straight times until he gets a smile out of me. He has my mother go to a fortune teller, and afterward he buys her a French beret from an old woman hawking them near the refreshment stands. I can finally see how much this day means to Voolich. He is rushing us like a frat pledge, needing to belong. Whether my mother has figured this out or not, I don't know.

He buys Wiley and me cheeseburgers, hands us ten-dollar bills for the arcade, ushers us to the men's room, all things he considers to be fatherly behavior. No matter how hard he tries, he isn't up to the easy confidence the task requires. I can't help but remember the last summer with my dad. He was lobbying hard then too, but at least he had actual charm on his side.

Voolich is shiny with flop sweat as he continues to drag us from one so-called attraction to another. The half-empty park seems to be shuttering to a halt before our eyes. The wind has picked up too, and now it's just a cold autumn day. Voolich's forced jauntiness only serves to accentuate the worst of all this. When he affects the posture and accent of the park's pirate mascot, we all know it's time to go home.

Back in the car, after we finally make our exit, I am almost content. Voolich's failure has been so complete and indisputable; he won't be around much longer. He'll be sent back to his gloomy life above Shoe Town. At least there's that. But on the way home, my mother, still wearing that idiotic beret, resumes their conversation about her exams as if nothing has happened, and Wiley sits next to me happily consumed with the Etch A Sketch he won at the roulette wheel. It suddenly occurs to me that they are going to forgive him. Worse yet, I see that they think there is nothing to forgive. Before we're on the road five minutes, Ma and Wiley each thank Voolich for giving us such a fine time, how it turned out perfect after all. I am stunned into silence until Ma turns around from the front seat and glares, forcing me to mumble something tolerable in Voolich's direction.

Then I slump back down in my seat, looking out the window for the rest of the drive as the South Shore drifts by. I sit there thinking about Ma's fierce optimism and her efforts to reinvent herself, how she has willed us all to move on and how she has pulled it off. And I think about Wiley's knee-jerk cheerfulness and how his perfect-little-man routine isn't a routine at all. I wonder how I've landed here among these people, like an alien spore in a science-fiction movie.

Ma doesn't marry Voolich. They remain friends for another year after Treasure Island, until he eventually stops coming around and hooks up with another woman, a cashier from his store. There will be other men in Ma's life, but nothing too serious, as far as I ever know. She prefers not to get tangled up with anyone else's dreams, she tells me once. She is devoted to her studies, getting her teacher's certificate, and taking more classes part time, eventually earning a doctorate in education and becoming an assistant principal at a high school in South Boston, before she retires happily to New Mexico, to a clean, whitewashed house on the edge of the desert with cottonwood trees and scorpions in her yard. She just turned eighty, volunteers at the local library, dabbles in watercolors, and still wears her hair too long. Wiley refers to her as "our bootleg Georgia O'Keeffe."

My brother will remain grounded and kind. Kindness is Wiley's special gift. It will follow him around for the rest of his life. He grows up to run a social service agency on the Cape, making a business out of his sweet nature and good intentions. He settles down with a wonderful guy named Grady, who sings in a bluegrass band, as if it's still the seventies. They adopt and raise three amazing kids, who I refer to as "Wiley's Embarrassment of Riches." He's a grandfather now. Like Ma often tells me, Wiley gives and gives, but he gets so much in return. But it's not until we are on our way back from Treasure Island in Voolich's car that I realize I'm not like them at all, with my high-strung nature and ticking complaints.

It's my father who I resemble. Not his swagger or smooth charisma, but the restlessness, the impatience, the always wishing for something better, and just out of reach, all of which will lead to my own failed marriages, an erratic sales career, and a grown daughter who rarely returns my calls. Sometimes I still imagine my dad standing over my bed the night before he leaves us for good. The need to start a new and different life is clinging to him like a wet sheet. Something is propelling him. It's not Delores, exactly, or the promise of sunny California, but it's something. And I can almost make out the jagged shape of it; feel its clumsy weight, as he backs out of my room for the very last time.

THE JOY FACTOR

Sarah sat in the kitchen surveying the blueberry scene in front of her. Dozens of pies, bread loaves, and muffin tins were stacked on the table. It was a July morning in a busy resort town on the coast of Maine. Sarah had been baking (on and off) for twenty-four hours. The air was thick and hot with the aroma of sizzled butter. There was an enormous mixing bowl on the floor that held the rejected berries, unripened or otherwise vetoed from the baking process. The sink was a jumble of dirty pans, spoons, and measuring cups. The countertop was a staging area for pie crusts made from scratch. Packing supplies were heaped perilously in the corner by the dishwasher.

The apartment was a summer sublet, an unremarkable two-bedroom space with bare white walls and simple furnishings. Sarah was renting the apartment from a Bowdoin professor of medieval studies, a woman who traveled to Europe during school breaks to research a book on religious iconography. The apartment sat above a busy souvenir shop, where in deference to the Maine tourist trade, a lobster theme had been incorporated into the design of nearly all the trinkets sold there, everything from key chains to pot holders.

Sarah had waited all summer to peddle these baked goods to tourists. The peak of the blueberry and tourist seasons had now coincided. Every spare moment of the previous week (when not waitressing at the Fishermen's Café), Sarah had been picking blueberries from the plentiful bushes along a hiking trail several miles from the center of town.

Her fingers were sore and stained purple.

Persis was still asleep. She was Sarah's roommate and had promised to help her box everything up, load the car, and transport the inventory to a congested intersection of the nearby coastal highway. There they planned to set up card tables and sell the blueberry stuff at seriously inflated prices. Persis hadn't taken part in any of the actual berry picking or preparation, but Sarah still counted on her assistance as a vendor. They went to the same college in Boston. Sarah would be a senior in September, finishing a political science major. Persis was a rising sophomore. She'd answered an ad for a summer share that Sarah had placed on a campus website. By splitting expenses, Sarah had hoped she could work a few less shifts at the café.

Sarah had discovered this town after reading an article about its seaside charm. Coming to work here for the summer was a better option than returning to her mother's gloomy apartment in a suburb of Boston—where an aura of unhappiness still drifted. Sarah spent as little time there as possible. The two previous summers she had remained at school, taking an elective or two while working at a chaotic Starbucks in Kenmore Square.

Nothing had been the same for Sarah's family since her father had died of a massive heart attack a week before her high school graduation. After his death, it was discovered that he had lost his job. He'd been a hospital administrator. There were accusations of embezzlement and an affair with a woman in his office. If he had lived, charges were to be filed. There was evidence of a sudden, blazing gambling addiction. The man had gone through everything—savings, college funds, and retirement accounts. He'd accumulated debts everywhere. The family home had to be sold immediately at a shortfall. Sarah, her mother, and her younger brother had moved to a modest apartment in the center of the same town where they had always lived, their misfortune now on display to a cross section of nosy friends and neighbors.

Three years later, Sarah was still in a complicated limbo of fury and sadness over her father's death. It was impossible for her to comprehend his spiraling, secret life. Her father had been kind and compassionate, a suburban Little League coach who liked crosswords and his outdoor grill. Sometimes he spoke in an old-fashioned, courtly manner, reciting random quotations or old song lyrics, charming everyone around the dinner table. Sarah simply could not accept what had happened. It was as if she'd never known the man at all. It had been even worse for her brother, who was only sixteen at the time. Jonah had been devoted to their dad since infancy. Sarah remembered their easy, jokey camaraderie, their fanatical devotion to the Boston sports teams, their misery over the Pats losing Tom Brady.

Jonah was reeling after their father's death. Soon he was spiraling himself, screwing up in school, raising hell with his friends, getting trashed almost every night. He'd somehow graduated from high school and was accepted to a small college in rural Pennsylvania, where his substance abuse had only accelerated. He was arrested seven months ago in the middle of his sophomore year—for disorderly conduct and possession of a large amount of oxycodone. He had avoided jail time but was given two hundred hours of community service. The charges also landed him in a court-mandated drug rehabilitation program near Philadelphia. That's where he still was. In June, from rehab, Jonah had written Sarah a letter. It was the first pen-and-paper communication she remembered ever receiving from her brother. Before she opened the envelope, she had shifted it from hand to hand, feeling the weight of its pages.

The clients at the rehab were not allowed to communicate by electronic device, Jonah explained. It was as if advanced technology was partly responsible for the clients' addictions. Jonah wrote about what a strange world it was in rehab, where you had to get up super early to attend group meetings and do chores, before you were allowed to eat or even take a shit. It was *discipline*, he explained, like in the army, except the clients were battling their own crazy addictions, and not foreign enemies. He thought it was working, the discipline thing. He wasn't *desperate* to get high anymore. His body felt better sober, he wrote. The painkillers had totally kicked his ass. He'd heard terrible stories in the rehab. The stories "had burned right into" him, he said, though he wasn't supposed to judge anyone else's "journey," which was how the counselors referred to the clients' "crooked, little lives." In the twelve-step meetings and in life, they wanted the addicts to give themselves over to a higher power, but at first Jonah didn't want any part of a god that would allow all the crappy things to happen in the world. Then he was told he could visualize the higher power any way he wanted. One of the guys there, for instance, pictured the sun and the moon and the stars. This was the part in the letter where Jonah had explained that he was envisioning his own higher power as their dead, disgraced father.

Sarah put the letter down and had taken a few deep breaths when she read that. When she picked up the letter again, Jonah was telling her that it wasn't as nuts or as pathetic as it sounded, because if their dad really was able to be the higher power, then maybe that's how he could fix things after how badly he'd fucked it all up. Maybe he could watch over them from beyond and see that their lives would basically be happy from here on out. That's what he hoped for, anyway, though he admitted there was a lot of twisted, false hope at the rehab. Jonah mentioned that he'd written a letter to their mother too, only with cleaner language, and without the news of their dad as the higher power because he figured she'd want to bang her head against the wall if she read that—something Sarah figured was probably true.

Sarah had responded to Jonah's letter immediately, providing her summer address, and insisting he come join her as soon as he was released. Guilt over Jonah's situation still throbbed in her like an infection. Sarah had left for college two months after their father's death—last-minute school loans had needed to be arranged. She had been grateful to go, but now it felt like she had fled a crime scene.

There was an alcove in the living room of the apartment where she could fit an air mattress, if he were to join her, or perhaps Jonah could sleep on the sofa. It had to be more comfortable than the boot camp atmosphere he had described and certainly more attractive than the option of traveling back home to their mother, who would hover over him like a forlorn security guard with her sad eyes and suspicious heart.

Sarah's mother had a demanding job now, as a program manager for the county rec department, and she worked night shifts in a bookstore, still chipping away at the debt with which she'd been left. She jogged and swam and attended a book club. This perpetual motion looked more like distraction to Sarah than a brand-new life, as if the woman was a living example of the slogan *Depression can't hit a moving target*. Sarah remembered how lighthearted her mother used to be, but that was before the shock and betrayal surrounding her husband's death. The woman who remained was a brisk and unhappy figure, poised for the next catastrophe.

Sarah heard Persis come out of her bedroom and walk down the hallway. She appeared in the kitchen wearing an oversized white T-shirt that came down to her knees. Persis washed out a pan in the crowded sink and went about the business of fixing her oatmeal, which consisted of many random ingredients. Persis preferred to stay silent in the mornings. She recited yoga mantras in her head and flashed distracted smiles around. She was quite petite, with delicate features and perfect bone structure. Her auburn hair cascaded to her shoulders, as if professionally tousled, even though she had just tumbled out of bed. Even in the harsh morning light, without a hint of makeup on her unwashed face, Persis was strikingly lovely. Sarah, who possessed a less conspicuous sort of attractiveness, was grateful that her roommate possessed no vanity and was somewhat oblivious to her smashing looks and the seismic impact they had on others.

At school, Persis was exclusively attracted to big, fearsome athletes, football types, guys who towered over her and looked as if they could hold her in the palm of their enormous hands. Her last boyfriend was a junior weightlifter with a long Polish name. He had transferred to

USC. Persis did not believe in long-distance relationships, so she had cast the weightlifter aside, urging him to take up with a more geographically appropriate California girl. He had been sending desperate texts all summer, pleading for reconciliation. Persis had carefully ghosted him. Sarah had never met the unhappy weightlifter, but she'd seen various online pictures of him, a predictably large, square-jawed titan. She was glad he was on the other side of the country and not within stalking distance. Sarah's own romantic experience was limited to a few timid high school boyfriends and one awkward Bumble hookup she didn't like to remember.

After she had moved in, Persis told Sarah that her parents thought she was in London for a study-abroad program, doing summer research on the English novel. They had sent her eight thousand dollars for the registration fee and travel expenses, no questions asked. Her parents were both busy corporate attorneys, so presumably this would not bankrupt them. Persis sent emails to them every few days detailing classes she was not attending and phantom visits to British landmarks, which she described with tidy narratives lifted off Wikipedia.

Sarah liked her roommate, even though she was ripping off her parents. She liked her loopy determination and breezy style. They didn't see each other much, given Sarah's work schedule and Persis's random pursuits. Persis exercised a lot. She hiked the rocky beaches and took hot yoga classes every day at a local studio. When they did socialize, Persis chattered on in an interesting fashion about the books she read (a slew of subjects, ranging from the history of ecoterrorism to an eight-hundred-page biography of Margaret Sanger) and certain aspects of her curious belief system. Sarah, however, would deflect even the most innocent questions floated in her direction. She had never told

Persis about her father's scandal, for instance, or her own sad and simmering reaction to it. She would have rather performed surgery on herself than explain any of that, though she did mention to Persis that Jonah might be joining them in Maine before too long.

Persis made some space across from Sarah and sat down at the table with her bowl of oatmeal. She lifted the spoon to her lips. Then she stared at the baked goods looming in front of her and asked Sarah in a gentle and enchanting tone, "So are we all set to move your motherfucking merchandise?"

The day was cloudless and nearly perfect. Perfect weather was unusual for this region of Maine, known for its short summers and arbitrary temperatures. Sarah and Persis traveled to the edge of the busy highway and set up the little business between a rest area dotted with pine trees and a gas station. They chose the southbound lane, hoping to entice the tourists departing the state to take home one last token of their time in Vacationland.

It was instantly apparent to Sarah that she could not have chosen a better sales partner than Persis. It was not only her good looks, which would have stopped the weekend traffic even if it wasn't already slowed to a crawl. It was how Persis displayed an attitude of serene confidence and glacial sincerity, as if she were a storybook princess or a seasoned diplomat. Even while selling pies on the side of a road, dressed in jeans and a crop top, she exuded a sense of understated glamour. The customers swiveled their necks to get a better look, as if she were a rare astronomical event. A state trooper who stopped by on a motorcycle to inquire about vendor permits left chastened and blushing after a few minutes' conversation with her. Sarah assumed it must be this quality of quiet largesse that had slayed the weightlifter and the others who had come before.

The sale was a rousing success. Shortly before 2 p.m., there were only a few more pies and muffin baskets remaining. They would clear a good deal of cash today, exceeding Sarah's expectations. Not for the first time that summer, Sarah imagined what it would be like if she left school and stayed on in Maine for good. There was something about the rugged coastline and sea air, the boats moored and bobbing dreamily in the harbor—the distance from her life in Boston. She'd met others in town who had dropped out of whatever they were doing to stay on. Mostly these folks were artists of some sort, muralists, glass blowers, candlemakers. There was a bit of an artist colony here. It was a hand-to-mouth existence, of course, and the winters, she was told, were rough and bleak, but there must be a certain dignity to enduring the off-season. Sarah was no artist, but she had ideas, like selling these baked goods, and she wondered if she might fashion herself into a small-town entrepreneur, a thrilling notion of escape and reinvention.

A BMW with a Massachusetts license plate pulled off the road just then. An attractive woman in her early forties peered out the passenger window and scanned the tables.

"Smart idea you have here," she declared, motioning to the highway, which right then resembled a parking lot. "Captive audience!"

A handsome, windblown man, in the style of an aging catalog model, was driving. He had the confident look of the successful professional about him, but he seemed somewhat exasperated at being coerced by his wife into buying overpriced pies from the side of the road. Sarah guessed he was a tax lawyer or an insurance executive or a cardiologist at Mass General. Perhaps he and his wife were both cardiologists with their own private practice. There was a gloss of wealth and privilege to these people that Sarah found vaguely annoying.

As she drew closer to the car, Sarah noticed there was a teenage girl staring out from the back seat. She had bright and inquisitive eyes and was sitting next to a boy of maybe twelve. The boy was deeply occupied playing a video game on the tablet in his lap, but the girl was taking everything in—the traffic, the sale items, the incomparable Persis. The husband perked up at the Persis development and leaned across his wife to toss out a few obvious remarks in her direction about the weather.

Impressively, Persis ignored the man.

Sarah locked eyes with the curious girl in the vehicle and almost immediately a memory emerged, bold and sharp. A car trip with her parents, after Sarah had turned fifteen. They had taken her to New York City in celebration of her birthday and stayed at a midtown hotel, where it was difficult to sleep for all the sirens and calamity rumbling outside. Jonah had been with them too, of course, but like the boy in the car, he had been oblivious to his natural surroundings and was consumed with *Call of Duty* most of the time.

On their second night in the city, they had attended a Broadway show, a megahit musical about teenage witches and warlocks. Sarah had been obsessed with the soundtrack back home, its lush, heartfelt ballads sung to perfection by a young and gifted cast. The show was Sarah's birthday present, the real reason they had all traveled to New York. Their seats were perfect, eighth-row center. The performance was mesmerizing, with a sustained and thunderous ovation at the curtain. Afterward, Sarah stood around in the theater's alley with other overwrought teenage fans as cast members departed from the stage door. It was a humid August night. Sarah's parents and Jonah stood off to the side, looking tired and sweaty and a little embarrassed for her.

When the actors emerged, one or two at a time (as if from a candy dispenser), they were accosted by the eager, swarming crowd. Sarah presented her Playbill to everyone who appeared, and all the performers complied with autographs, though with varying degrees of graciousness and enthusiasm. After scoring the signatures, Sarah excitedly rejoined her family, and then they began to thread their way through the Times Square hordes. They walked past another theater on the same block, which housed a revival of a Tennessee Williams play with an all-star, award-winning cast. A massive advertisement on its marquee displayed a quote from a famous critic.

See this show, the critic admonished, *or live to regret it forever!*

Sarah stopped short and blinked at the ad. The threat and sadness in that statement bewildered her. Angry pedestrians were forced to weave around where she stood frozen in place. She kept staring at the critic's words as they seared her teenage brain. It was the idea of missing something *so* important that you would regret it for *your whole, entire life*. This left her with a sense of loss that ached in her like a wound. Her father had turned around and come back to see what was wrong. In a small, strangled voice, Sarah had tried to explain. And when she did this, he had not grown impatient or yanked her along, as other fathers surely would have. In fact, he'd been wonderfully attentive and sympathetic, carefully listening to her desperate thoughts, even as the crowds continued to shove by them.

"Ah, my smart, sensitive girl," her father had whispered to her, in the funny, old-fashioned lilt he sometimes used, "this is something to ponder. I have always loved the way your mind works! I can't wait to see all the ways in which you will conquer the world."

Her father always believed in Sarah's potential, as if he saw it shooting out of her fingertips. He could see straight into her heart and he understood her better than anyone else. That night, his patience and validation made Sarah nearly weep with gratitude. He had swung his arm around Sarah's shoulders in the casual and comforting way that was his habit back then, when his troubles, whatever they might have been, were still hidden from view. They had stood there on the sidewalk until Sarah composed herself, and then they had joined her mother and brother and walked back to the hotel.

The woman in the BMW decided to buy the rest of the pies, and so Sarah quickly shifted her attention. She took the woman's cash and gave her back the change. Persis began packing it all up in her offhand, luminous style. As the transaction was completed and the car drove away, Sarah found herself worrying in a loose but visceral way about the girl in the back seat and her lovely-looking family. The world was such a perilous place. It could come crashing down on you at any moment.

Then, as if on cue, she looked up to see Jonah racing toward her across the highway, dodging through the stop-and-go congestion. He had spotted his sister from the northbound lane, just as he was cursing the summer traffic. He'd parked on the shoulder and then come galloping.

"Sarah, Sarah, Sarah," Jonah yelled, horns blaring as he sprinted across the road. He continued calling her name as he got to her, picked her up, and swung her around.

There must have been some weight lifting privileges at the rehab,

Sarah thought. Jonah was so strong and fit. When she pulled away from his hug, she could see that her brother's face had cleared up now. His skin was rosy again and unblemished. He had lost the gaunt, ravaged look of the previous three years.

Jonah was back.

"Why didn't you call or text?" Sarah asked, happily pounding his shoulders. "I had no idea you were on your way."

"I have no phone." Jonah shrugged.

Sarah had forgotten about the *no electronics* decree at the rehab.

"A new buddy of mine has another sixty days down there," Jonah told her, "so he let me borrow his car. I plugged your address into his GPS and started driving. I left at five a.m. and only stopped once to take a leak."

"I'm so happy to see you!" Sarah said. "Happier than you can imagine."

And she meant it. Her voice wavered and broke. She felt unhinged. She was smiling through tears.

"I thought I was hallucinating when I spotted you. I almost crashed into the Prius in front of me," Jonah said. "What's going on here, anyway?"

He was motioning to the nearly empty card tables, the remaining inventory.

"Sale of the century," Sarah said. "Long story. Or really not so long."

Jonah had stopped listening. Persis, having retreated during the reunion, had now stepped forward again. Jonah registered her presence with a triple-espresso jolt.

"This is Persis, my summer roommate," Sarah said, introducing them. "Persis, this is Jonah."

Jonah stammered out an unintelligible greeting.

"Ah, yes," Persis said. "The brother."

*

Later that evening, after they had all pitched in to clean up the kitchen, Sarah ordered takeout food from the café and they sat on the sofa watching Sarah's favorite television show, an entire real-life series devoted to individuals who had survived abductions by serial killers. It was terrifying to think there were enough of these folks to create a show around. On each episode, there were dramatic re-creations and riveting interviews that focused on how specific victims managed to survive gunshots or knife wounds or brutal assaults.

The show fascinated her.

Jonah and Persis did not find it so enthralling. They made fun of the program's dour host and insulted the dramatic re-creations. In fact, they lobbed sarcastic comments throughout.

"Who are we supposed to be rooting for here?" Persis quipped as this episode's victim, an indignant and not entirely sympathetic Kansas businessman, was being interviewed.

"Yeah," Jonah chimed in, "I'd like to hear the psycho's version of what actually went down."

They were laughing loudly. It irritated Sarah that they disliked a show she loved so much and that they were being so cynical and jokey about real-life mayhem too. She would have expected Jonah to appreciate a program about survivors more— and she had never seen Persis act so playful or silly. There was something else too. Sarah sensed a kind of electric current at work here, the swell of barometric pressure in the room, as these two slammed the show and snuck appreciative glances at each other behind Sarah's back.

She might have predicted this would happen, though despite being tall and good-looking, Sarah's brother was not exactly in the Persis wheelhouse. He played baseball when he was little and some high school lacrosse, before missing too many practices and getting cut from the team. But Jonah had never been your standard, hulking jock. Then his drug use had thinned him out and dissipated him. However, this healthier, beefier version of her little brother who had shown up was perhaps a more likely object of her roommate's affection.

After the show, Persis stretched theatrically and announced that she was going off to bed. She glanced briefly at Jonah as she said this. Sarah wondered if there was a secret message in that look.

Wait an hour and then come to me after your sister falls asleep.

"Cool girl," Jonah said, nodding in Persis's direction as she left the room.

"Yep, that's right," Sarah answered. "A cool . . . and slightly peculiar girl."

She said these words extra slowly and used a singsong tone. Jonah laughed. Sarah had her brother stand up while she put sheets on the sofa. He was fine with the sleeping arrangements. He said he would have gladly slept on the floor. After Sarah was finished, Jonah dropped back down and started flipping channels.

Sarah stood over her brother, watching him carefully.

"Are you really okay, Jonah?" she asked.

There was a lot riding on this simple question, and she suddenly worried that she might start to cry again.

Jonah hesitated before answering.

"I think so," he said, glancing up at her.

Sarah bit her lip. What else could he be expected to say?

"I mean, I can't promise anything," Jonah continued, "and I need to find a meeting up here, NA or AA, something, but yeah, I'm okay. For today at least. You know, one of the guys in my afternoon group, a truck driver with a fentanyl habit, talked about everyday joy all the time. He referred to it as the joy factor and described it as that extra-special something that keeps us all going in this world. In his case, it was the way his kid smiles at him when he gets home after a cross-country haul. That smile is what made him want to stop doing the drug. I think about that. I'm not sure what my own ordinary joy would even look like, but I guess it's healthy that I've been wondering about it. I do know that I want my life back."

Then Sarah really was crying. She turned away from her brother before her tears turned into ugly sobs, while Jonah, looking slightly embarrassed, went back to fussing with the remote.

He had forgotten his toothbrush, so Sarah found him an extra one. Then she handed him a towel and warned him about the lousy water pressure. They took turns in the bathroom and then Sarah headed to her room and crawled into bed. She hoped she could drift off quickly. She didn't want to hear her brother as he snuck down the hall to Persis or any other sounds once he got there. She knew she should be worried about Jonah's involvement with her roommate. He was just out of rehab, after all, and vulnerable. There were probably rules about these things, but after the events of the day and his surprise arrival, she wanted to be hopeful.

Tomorrow she would call her mother. Jonah had agreed to that. The poor woman didn't even know her son was out of rehab. Sarah thought she should ask her up here for a visit. She had been considering this since that memory of her father in New York City had washed over her. Her mother couldn't help her fretting and wistful love—or the leftover sorrow in her eyes either. It was not fair, Sarah thought, to keep the woman at arm's length simply because nobody wanted to be reminded of the past or what they'd all lost or because none of them had found a way to move on. Only Jonah had started that process, Sarah thought, the only one in meaningful recovery.

This reminded her of Persis again, her stunning beauty and mystifying ways. Jonah might benefit from a full-on flirtation with someone like that. Sarah thought about their instant, blazing chemistry. Suddenly the idea of Jonah and Persis together pleased her enormously. As she stared up at the shadowy ceiling, Sarah thought again of her father and what Jonah had written from rehab about him, how he was maybe watching over them all. This was not something Sarah believed or perhaps even wanted, but she would be willing to discuss it with her brother in the morning—or for however long he was planning to stay.

OFF THE GRID

Sam, my husband, comes into our apartment with a bloody lip and a triumphant lilt to his voice. Before he's even through the door, he's telling me about a fight he just got into on the subway. I get up from the sofa and pull him under the overhead light in the living room to get a better look. I take his face in my hands. His lip is split open, a jagged crimson trail, but the wound isn't too bad. There's some blood on his cheek too, where he must have smeared it. I've dealt with a lot of calamity in my life, so this doesn't exactly panic me, though it surprises me some. Sam's not usually the scrappy type. He doesn't even like action movies and has been known to close his eyes at anything particularly gruesome that comes on television. These are qualities I've come to admire. He tells me that he accidentally jostled some idiot on a crowded R train and that the guy freaked out on him.

"I apologized for bumping into him, Katie," Sam says. "I was totally sincere."

"And what did he say?" I ask.

"'Fuck off.' That's what he said."

"Wow. That's not too friendly."

"No, it isn't! So I told him to calm down, and that's when he starts talking more crap, but at the same time he's also looking me up and down, like he's sizing me up. I figure maybe he's going to back off, because I must have had a good four inches and thirty pounds on the guy and he was definitely older too, like maybe even fifty. I had my arms folded, scowling down at him, just shaking my head in response—and that's when he socked me in the mouth."

"Jesus," I say. "Then what happened?"

"Well, I hit him back. I shoved him hard and we stumbled up against the subway doors. I had him by the collar of his shirt. By that time, everybody in the car had their phones out and were filming us, and some old lady kept muttering 'The world we live in' in a really annoying way. When we pulled into Times Square, as soon as the doors slid open, the asshole pulled away from me, ripping his shirt in the process, and ran out into the crowd."

Sam's eyes are very bright. He's bouncing on the balls of his feet. He looks pumped up and victorious.

"My hero," I want to say, but I'm afraid it will sound vaguely sarcastic, so I just ask him if he thinks any of this will show up on YouTube.

"Doubt it. By the time people started recording, it was basically over."

I can tell he wants me to say something else, something commemorative and jolly.

"Another win for the good guys" is what I come up with, but this hits my ear funny, and afterward Sam is still looking at me with a kind of eager expectation.

I think I should just stay quiet for a minute. I give him a hug instead, squeezing his biceps and patting his rear. I let out a sexy little grunt. This pleases him, I notice, and is probably more along the lines of what he's looking for. He grins happily, wincing through the bloody lip, and then he goes to the bathroom to clean himself up.

Later, I can't help but think about my old boyfriend Nick, who was known to get into some skirmishes. A stranger's critical glance or surly tone could set him off. He was sometimes on the lookout for trouble. Sometimes he found it. I can imagine what he would have done if somebody had told him to chill out on the subway. He was a bouncer when I met him, at a crummy club on the Lower East Side. I was one of the cocktail servers. Nick didn't last there too long. In my experience (I'd worked in a number of similar places), a good bouncer knows how to defuse situations and not stir the shit up. I hadn't slept with anyone in that club before Nick, including Cal, the manager, who was always pestering me about messing around. Cal thought he was irresistible and liked to believe he had his pick of all the females in the place, staff and patrons alike. He might have given me a better schedule or other perks if I'd looked his way, but I wasn't interested. He thought this was a big joke that I wouldn't hook up with him, that it was some sort of performance on my part, some kind of protracted foreplay. When he was in a lively mood, Cal made a lot of jokes about our *sexual destiny*, and when he wasn't, he'd call me Miss Priss and make me clean the horrible bathrooms.

"Someday," he'd say as I was cashing out at the end of my shifts, "you'll see."

Then he'd wag his tongue at me in a lewd way. I've had worse managers, believe it or not.

Sam and I go over to Joe and Ivy's for dinner. We walk there in the pleasant June twilight. Sam is holding my hand, but his arm is swinging, as if the adrenaline from the subway incident is still coursing through him. Sam has known Joe and Ivy since college. They live about a half mile from us in Queens on the first floor of a nice house, with their three-year-old son, Zane. This is an old Italian neighborhood. There's a lot of religious statuary placed in well-tended gardens. In December, the streets will explode with Christmas lights, ten-foot Santas, and flashing nativities.

When Joe opens the door, he takes one look at Sam's swollen lip and shouts, "What happened to you, bro?" which brings Ivy running in from the kitchen.

Joe grabs my husband by the chin and squints at the injury. He makes a few cracks in my direction about spousal abuse, waving his finger at me in mock outrage, until Ivy shoots him a heated glance. Then they both look worried, as if Joe may have put his foot in it, as if I really am the one who clobbered my husband. They haven't known me too long (Sam and I dated less than six months and have only been married for four), and I'm not sure what Sam has told them about my *colorful* past or how much any of it bleeds through on its own. Who knows what they really think? The awkwardness doesn't last long, because Sam is launching into the story for them with even more gusto than he did with me.

I notice some details change this time through. In this version, the man on the subway is angrier and more foulmouthed, younger, and fit. And after getting popped in the mouth, Sam says he knocked the guy flat and that some of the passengers congratulated him for taking on a bully. This exaggeration isn't entirely consistent with Sam's personality, but it strikes me as particularly male, that mixture of bravado and audacity, that cocktail of embellishment. The next time I hear this story he might be dodging gunfire. I can't really begrudge Sam his time in the spotlight or his giddy bluster either. It's the first time he's taken a swing at anyone since middle school, and in his job running the HR department for a snooty architecture firm, he has to set an example of cool detachment and restraint.

Later we order takeout and sit around the living room while Sam gets on the floor with Zane, constructing a wooden train set. They spread tracks and tunnels everywhere, winding under our legs and leading all the way out into the kitchen. Zane has his own design in mind.

"No—that goes *here*," he says when Sam strays too far from the concept.

Sam is cheerful and accommodating. He's had all that practice working with those exacting architects. Also, maybe it's his way of showing me what a laid-back, hands-on dad he could be. Sam and I haven't nailed down the kid question yet, which everyone says you should do *before* you get married. It still floats and dances between us like pollen, though I think Sam feels optimistic about his powers of persuasion. He's crazy about kids. The issue isn't a deal-breaker for me. I just turned twenty-nine (Sam's a year younger), so luckily we're not at that breathless urgency stage yet. The truth is, I am not naturally maternal and have never put much faith in the idea of a family unit, probably because of the haphazard way my siblings and I were raised by our bitter, periodically abusive parents. My brothers and sisters all scattered like dandelion seeds as soon as they got the chance to leave rural Pennsylvania, just like I did. The less said about that part of my life the better.

I do admire Joe and Ivy's nesty vibe, even if their apartment sometimes resembles the aftermath of a birthday party at Chuck E. Cheese. I get along well with them too. They have the fizzy, eager-to-please personalities of fundraisers for struggling nonprofits, which is what they both are, though raising a toddler in a tiny space has probably flattened out some of that greedy energy and changed their priorities, making them easier to be around. They have been a couple since their freshman year. Sam was Joe's roommate. I am amused when they are together like this and get around to reminiscing about their school days, their wild keg parties and midnight skinny-dipping, how hungover they were for certain midterms, et cetera. They get a little buzz from admiring their bolder, younger selves. I appreciate the innocence of these recollections and only occasionally do the stories annoy the shit out of me. I was leading a very different kind of life when I was that age.

I'd been on my own in the city since I was seventeen, living in bombed-out apartments with roommates who were either broke-ass morons or your standard lost souls. One winter I spent a couple of weeks in a homeless shelter after the girl I was rooming with had a psychotic break, smashing all the windows in our apartment and shaving off her eyebrows. Then there was the time I crashed with a bunch of squatters in Alphabet City for a while. This was not something I'd recommend to anyone. One of the squatters overdosed and died right in front of me. She was a girl my age, a runaway from Connecticut, who called herself Gem and had a daisy tattooed on the back of her neck. I was the one who called 911 that night, on somebody's stolen phone, after she'd swallowed her tongue and turned blue.

Mostly back then, I served drinks at illegal clubs and after-hours parties, even when I was underage. I also worked for a few months as a dancer in Brooklyn, in a shoddy place near the Gowanus Canal. The patrons there were a weary group, sad and twitchy.

"You're providing a service," the no-nonsense owner used to tell us (straight-faced) as if we were clinical social workers. In that spirit, I did try to listen to the customers' problems, when I wasn't dancing, when it was my job to get them to buy me watered-down drinks.

Sam knows about these things, though I usually just offer up a slightly sanitized version of my past. For instance, I stick to the funny stories about my dancing days (there were a few of these—mostly at the expense of the customers) and I stay clear of the miserable, depressing part. And I haven't told him about the time I was an escort for all of about thirty minutes, because what's to be gained from that? Though Sam doesn't know *all* the details of my personal history, he knows enough of them. If anything, he romanticizes me as a survivor more than he should. I feel pretty removed from those days, actually—when I was living a sort of throwaway life, and then later when I had my time with Nick, who swept me along for a while.

Here's the story: The night I was introduced to Nick, right after he was hired, my eyesight momentarily fogged up and blurred, like I was experiencing some kind of hysterical blindness. His confident swagger and fuck-it-all attitude made me weak in the knees. He made me swoon like a ditz in a movie. Nick was handsome, but not as good-looking as some of the other guys in the club. So, it wasn't just that. I could see immediately this was someone who could take care of himself, not only because of his size and the fact that he was a bouncer. He just looked resilient to me and wised-up. Unwavering. That's how I read him, anyway, and these were traits I also recognized in myself. I was so flustered that first night, screwing up drink orders whenever he glanced in my direction. A few times when he caught my eye, he held up his hand in greeting and flashed a crooked grin. Nick wasn't being subtle or coy or playing any games. I liked that.

It was on.

"Get your head in the game, Katie," Cal snapped at me a few times, noticing all this.

Nick waited around for me that first night, after my shift was over. It took me a long time to cash out, and then I had to help Eduardo, our dyslexic bartender, with the inventory, another one of Cal's little punishments.

"I was ready to put out an Amber Alert on you," Nick said when I finally left the building, as he came up to me on the sidewalk. "Where were you, anyway?"

"Living the dream," I told him.

The crooked smile again.

And then he walked me all the way home to where I was living at the time, in Hell's Kitchen, on a tenement block that hadn't been overhauled yet. I was back with the same roommate who'd broken all the windows, but now it was years later and she'd had some treatment. She was sane again, more or less, and her eyebrows had grown back. She was selling perfume at Macy's and stayed most nights with her boyfriend, a guy who roamed Times Square dressed up like a cartoon character and got tips for taking photos with tourists.

The apartment was an illegal sublet, a terrible fifth-floor walk-up. I remember Nick made some leering joke along the lines of "Stairway to Heaven" as we made our way up there. But when we got inside, we didn't fall on top of each other or anything. I made us some scrambled eggs and we continued the conversation from our walk, stories about our lives up until then that seemed to overlap and link up. Later, we washed the dishes and then turned in like an old married couple, but once we got to bed, we had a nice, lively time.

Nick lasted a couple months at the club before there was such an uptick in fights and squabbles at the door that he was let go.

"This isn't the WWE," Cal told him the night he was fired. "You need to get your shit together, man."

I knew enough to stay out of it. I was just pleased that Nick left peacefully without breaking Cal's neck. He was aware that Cal had a thing for me, another reason for him to hate the guy's guts. Later, in my apartment, he rattled off a complicated list of reprisals, which I had a time dissuading him from carrying out. The next week Nick came to the club to meet me after work, and that's when things took a turn.

"What's this?" Cal said when he saw Nick sitting at the bar.

I had about ten minutes left of my shift.

"He just came to walk me home, Cal," I replied. "We'll be out of here in five minutes."

"He'll be out of here right now, Katie," Cal told me. "He's not welcome."

"You can't do that," I said. "He's a paying customer."

"I can do what I want. This is my place."

"Actually, it's *not* your place," I said sharply. "You're just one of the managers."

The owner was a smartly dressed old man with rumored mob connections who rarely came around, and when he did show up, you had to serve him cooking sherry in a wineglass. But this was probably the wrong tone to take with Cal, who'd been jealous of Nick since he'd witnessed the connection between us that first night. Eduardo and a few of the other waitresses were gathered now, wondering what was about to happen, hoping for some bedlam to end the evening. Nick was watching too, from his end of the bar, coiled and biding his time. I could almost feel the heat rising off him across the room. We'd been together long enough for me to witness his flashes of anger out in the world. A few days before this, I'd pulled him off a guy he thought had stared at me too long on the street.

"Since when do you give me orders, Katie?" Cal said furiously. "I decide who comes and who goes. He goes. And if you don't like it, you can go too. Permanently."

Everyone was staring. I knew I only had a moment before all hell would break loose, before Nick would pounce on Cal and then Eduardo would be swinging the baseball bat he kept under the cash register. The new bouncer, a huge Russian, would get involved, and the cops might even be called, which would complicate things because Nick had told me there was a warrant out on him due to a missed court appearance. An earlier arrest for disorderly conduct. His explanation about that incident was murky, but now it was going through my mind. I had to make a decision fast.

"It's not fucking worth it," I finally said, as much to myself as to the others. "I'm outta here."

I reached behind the bar and grabbed my purse.

"Nice knowing y'all," I hollered.

It's not like I loved that job, but I was one of Cal's best servers, certainly the soberest and most dependable one. And behind all the dirty propositions, I think Cal liked me too, though this hadn't occurred to me until that moment when I saw the regret in his eyes. He wouldn't be able to back down, though, not in front of the rest of the staff or Nick, who was smiling lethally at him as he put his arm around me and we marched out of the club.

When we got out onto the sidewalk, Nick was euphoric.

"Baby, I can't believe you did that!" he said. "I just can't fucking believe it. You walked out on that dick. Did you see his face? His jaw was hitting the floor!"

Nick kept coming back to that theme for the rest of the night—my sacrifice on his behalf, which is how he saw it. Later, back at my apartment, when we made love, he was sweeter and more solicitous than usual, going down on me for a good, long while, which hadn't been one of his go-to activities before. My motivations for quitting the club hadn't so much been loyalty to Nick as avoiding a risky, pointless brawl, but it felt good to be appreciated nonetheless. I knew Nick had never been put first or defended before. He'd been raised by a scam-artist mother who had some serious drug and alcohol issues. They'd moved all over when he was young. Nick told me he'd been shoplifting and begging on the street from the time he was very small, hustling one way or another.

"You don't even want to know all the shit we got into," he said.

But he'd told me enough of it.

After I quit the bar, Nick started watching me with laser-like affection. His gratitude washed over me like a hot spring. It swelled around us like music. This experience was new to me (my relationship history was as sketchy as my résumé) and it scared me too, the idea that this was meant to happen, that perhaps we'd found each other out of everyone else in the world. In this rush of dreamy optimism, I had Nick move in (he'd been living on somebody's sofa in Bed-Stuy), which didn't please my roommate, who distrusted him on sight. She left soon after, to live with the guy in the Pokémon outfit, but at least she didn't break anything before she walked out.

I guess it was a relatively happy time, but neither one of us was working, so we had to solve the more practical concerns. I didn't want to go back to another skeevy club. I found a straight waitressing job instead, at a diner that looked just like the inside of a railroad car. Train memorabilia covered the walls. There was a crossing signal at the entrance. The waitresses were all dressed like conductors, with change-makers on our hips. It wasn't far from the UN. We got a lot of tourists in there. They were usually quite friendly, though their English was often fractured and they didn't always know how to tip.

Lucas, some old grifter buddy of Nick's, hired him for his moving company. It was just some brawny guys with a paneled truck. All off the books. People didn't know how to tip in that business either. Nick and his crew once got an extra five dollars (total!) from a young couple after moving their furniture up seven flights. The elevator was out of order, and it was the height of summer. Nick often came home fuming about clueless, stingy New Yorkers, sharing some unpleasant anecdote about a member of the general public he'd come in contact with at his job. One time some guy put his toddler on top of a heavy table Nick and Lucas were carrying because he thought it would make a cute photo on Facebook.

"It was like he thought his son was some little king and we were the fucking flunkies hoisting him around on a throne!" Nick seethed.

"Yuck," I replied. "But no one is really thinking straight during a move. Maybe he didn't mean anything by it."

This was a theory Nick refused to acknowledge. I began to wonder how he kept his temper all day, until I realized he was probably blowing up all over the place. It was a slapdash business designed for people who wanted to move on the cheap, and Lucas, the boss, liked him. There must have been a lot of latitude on that job.

I liked early mornings with Nick the best, before we had to get up, before the day's experiences wore him down. He'd curl around me drowsily in bed after we made love and talk about a future when we didn't have to work so hard.

"Someday we'll live in a better place than this, Katie, and not have to knock ourselves out just to make the rent. We'll be able to stay in bed all day long if we want."

I was surprised to hear such optimistic daydreams coming out of Nick. Circumstances didn't change just because you wanted them to, not in my experience. It took a lot to transform a life, like a winning Powerball ticket. The way I saw it, we were lucky to be living in this place, with the bathtub in the kitchen and roach traps covering the surfaces of everything. I'd been knocking around the city a long time by then. Expectations were just disappointments waiting to happen. That was my philosophy, if anything was.

On some of those cozy mornings, Nick told me that he wanted to show me Arizona, where he and his mother had lived for a while during one of her less larcenous and druggy periods. She actually had a real job for a time, at a hotel. Nick was in middle school then and he'd made a few friends. On the weekends, he and his mother would travel around the state in a Pontiac convertible, a car his mom had swindled out of some ex-boyfriend. These were his best memories of her. Nick still remembered the sandstone formations in Sedona and how their shades of orange glowed and flared at sunset. I liked hearing about this younger, happier Nick. His voice was soft when he told me about those times. There was almost a spiritual connection he still felt about the desert. This was different from the sexy, volatile guy I'd originally fallen for. Having to make room for both of these versions in my brain was how most people probably conducted a real relationship, but I was still a novice in this regard.

My manager at the diner was a pain in the ass, but within the normal restaurant parameters, with none of Cal's lecherous advances. He mostly just wanted us to pick up the pace. I liked the other waitresses there. It was a wholesome group, compared to what I was used to. A few of the girls were struggling actresses, pretty and upbeat. Others were going to school at night, wanting to be lawyers or bankers. I watched them all with a keen intensity, wondering how they'd arrived at their particular paths and how I'd arrived at mine. This was more on my mind, once Nick started stealing from his job, and then later, when everything began to slip.

The whole crew was stealing, as it turned out. It was something Lucas encouraged—take an item or two from every move. They tried to be clever and stay clear of electronics and expensive jewelry. They'd walk off with random stuff like bookends, salad bowls, a place setting or two. If there was an accusation, Lucas would say these things had been lost in transit or had never been there in the first place. People were less likely to bitch about the cheaper, less personal objects, if they noticed them missing at all. Our apartment became the holding facility for all this stuff, before it could be transferred to the pawnshop in midtown where Lucas's uncle worked. Our place began to resemble a neighborhood flea market. I hated the clutter almost as much as the needless risk we were taking.

When I complained about the mess, Nick would say, "Fuck me, Katie, for trying to bring more cash in, so maybe you could work a few less shifts!"

But I never saw any of that cash. Nick had started staying out after work, partying with Lucas and the guys. The extra money was probably going to that. Nick was sober when I met him, though I knew there were some nasty, shitfaced stories in his past. He'd blamed the disorderly conduct arrest on a weekend binge, for instance, and there was another time when he'd woken up after a blackout in a drunk tank upstate. Working in so many bars and clubs, I'd seen more examples of sloppy drunkenness and straight-up addiction than you could count. And watching Gem, the squatter, dragged around by the fussy and irritated EMTs, as if she was garbage, had a real effect on me too. After that, I wouldn't even sip a beer or try anything else. My life, I figured, was already challenging enough.

I might not have started up with Nick if he hadn't been sober when we met, but our attraction was so powerful, its impact so blazing and new, I might have taken my chances anyway. I wasn't really much for hypotheticals. Now I had a situation on my hands. Nick was coming home trashed and reeling every night, his hard-living friends probably egging him on. He never got particularly violent, at least, which was one thing to be thankful for, given his bumpy interactions in the world, but I'd still have to quiet him down when he'd stumble in. I'd have him drink tall glasses of water, one after another, make him down a few Advil, hand him slices of white bread to chew and swallow. I knew how to sober people up and stave off hangovers from my time in the bars. I'd help Nick take off his clothes, and then I'd put a bucket by his side of the bed.

In the mornings, he'd be contrite, making the promises that sobered-up drunks usually made. It was easier to believe him than to think we were falling into some miserable pattern together. But that's exactly what happened. It was a quick spiral. I might find Nick passed out in the bathroom, sprawled across the toilet, when I came home from a double shift. I'd have to drag him out of the way if I needed to pee. Or he might be sitting at the kitchen table having a slurry argument with a cereal box or he'd have burned the bottom out of a frying pan and left the gas on. I started dreading climbing the stairs every night. I had no idea what version of Nick I'd encounter, or if he'd even be conscious. I was grateful when he wasn't there at all, though I'd still worry if it got to be four a.m. and he wasn't home. Nick had one of those pay-as-you-go phones, which he rarely answered after a certain hour.

At work, the other waitresses talked about their auditions or mid-term exams, their plans for the future. They might complain about their boyfriends or husbands, but it was usually good-natured and often led to some other story about devotion and thoughtfulness. I'd listen to accounts of apple-picking weekends or trips to the shore, trembling with resentment. I was in a complicated limbo of exhaustion and fury. Nick was still functioning as a mover, where his loose, irregular hours probably played to his advantage. He'd cite his dependable work ethic whenever I suggested he had a problem. He'd get pissed off when I told him he needed to get some help.

"You don't know anything about this, Katie!" he'd shout. "I go to work every day just like you. You think you're better than me because you don't need to let off any steam or unwind after work. It's normal to kick back. Not everyone's a fucking ice queen like you, not everybody's a stuck-up little princess!"

This was similar to the shaming way Cal had spoken to me when he was trying to get me into bed, but I knew it was only Nick's denial talking. I'd hardly been leading a royal existence. Nick might never face his issues or seek any help. His mother had died of cirrhosis of the liver when he was nineteen and you could bet he didn't want to be lumped into any comparisons with her. He so vilified the woman in his non-desert stories that I often pictured her with a target on her back.

There were times, like after Nick puked all over the sofa or when he'd wet the bed and soak the mattress, that I'd scream and holler and threaten. I was going to throw him out, I'd say, if he didn't pull it together. I was going to call the cops and have him taken away. But I never did that. We'd been together nearly two years by then, and the recent scenes were all mixed up in my head with thoughts of Nick's awful childhood and the hopeful boy he'd been as he watched those shifting colors in Sedona. When he was sober, we continued to get along, more or less. We still made love some mornings. Our desire still cut deep. I suppose my reluctance to toss him out was tied up with my own disposable, off-the-grid existence in the city, where I'd always been a few bad choices away from the streets and catastrophe myself. I was only twenty-six when it started to go bad with Nick, when my life began to recede like the tide. A new one was looming, forming around me. If I tried, I could almost make out its ugly, jagged shape. My future felt written out for me.

But I was wrong about my future; because one afternoon during a freak spring snowstorm, Nick was killed by a taxicab that hopped a curb on Forty-Second Street. He was cold sober at the time. I had to go identify his body in a hospital on Tenth Avenue. Some nurse gave me directions to the morgue, but then I got lost in the bowels of the place. A janitor found me wandering the hallways, acting as if I'd been clubbed over the head. When I got home that night, I sat in a chair and watched the front door, waiting for Nick to walk in and tell me it had all been a joke. I'd never been someone who couldn't accept the reality of a situation, but the grief must have temporarily short-circuited that area of my brain. I was afraid to look in the mirror afterward too, so worried that I'd see some sign of relief or liberation on my face, but there was none of that. I was distraught and probably in shock. A couple days later Lucas came over and handed me an envelope with seven thousand dollars in it—Nick's cut, he said, from their recent drug deals. They'd apparently been selling oxycodone and fentanyl from out of the moving van. I knew nothing about that. Lucas must have thought I did. I wondered if Nick might have been using these painkillers too, mixing them with the alcohol, accelerating his own troubles. But it didn't make any difference now. I took the money. I needed it for Nick's cremation. There was really no one else but me to arrange anything. I was grateful to Lucas, who might have pocketed the cash, though the cynical part of me wondered whether Nick was owed a larger share or if Lucas expected more gratitude from me than I was prepared to offer. He lingered a little too long in the apartment, I'd thought.

I didn't have an actual funeral service for Nick, and the only time I really cried (ugly, wailing sobs) was when I spread his ashes in Fort Tryon Park, by a cluster of trees near the Cloisters. There was a view of the Hudson. It was a lovely spot, but I was crying because I thought if I was a better person, I would have flown to Arizona, rented a car, and driven to Sedona to spread Nick's ashes there, his favorite place in the universe. I told myself Nick would understand that I needed to keep most of this money for myself.

One of the waitresses from the restaurant helped me find an apartment in Astoria (her aunt was a rental broker who waived her fee) in a nice building near the elevated train. It was a sunny one-bedroom with polished, wide-plank floors, new appliances, and access to a garden in back. The stolen stuff had all been disposed of by then, and I gave away all of Nick's things. I got rid of everything I owned too: furniture, dishes, clothes. I moved to the new apartment and started all over with new possessions. I painted the walls a linen white and kept them bare. I wanted everything in my life to be simple and clear. I found a job at a nicer restaurant, on the Upper East Side, and took a class in hospitality management. I'm the day manager there now.

Sam lived in my new neighborhood, and we'd often see each other as we waited for the subway. It was a month before he worked up the nerve to talk to me and then it was only about random topics, like when he mentioned some nature documentary he'd seen. Sam could rattle off the group names of birds as if he was reciting a poem—a kit of pigeons, a host of sparrows, a company of parrots, and so forth. It was a surprise when I found this so charming, but I did, like most of our other interactions, and so we started going out. Sam was smart, with a square jaw and perfect posture. He had a gentle humor that sometimes turned dark, and he was honest and direct without being too blunt. He'd make eye contact and was polite with panhandlers, even when he wasn't handing anything over. I liked his cheery enthusiasm in bed too.

Sam was unhappy I'd had such a tough time in the world and said he was drawn to my durable heart. I told him a little bit about Nick, but not everything. Sam might have thought that he needed to *save* me, but he was wrong about that part. He was a boy from Minnesota whose mother still sent him care packages of brownies and new socks. I knew he was the right person for me before I fell in love with him, and when that piece fell into place, I surprised myself some more. We got married and then he moved in.

"It was fun tonight," Sam says when we leave Joe and Ivy's, as he takes my hand and we start the walk home.

"Yes," I say, "that's true."

It's a lovely summer Friday on the streets of the city. There's zero humidity this evening, and I can hear the soothing hum and rattle of the N train in the distance. Sam is talking to me about some comet, some upcoming astronomical event that won't happen again in our lifetimes. *Our lifetimes.* I am once again reminded of Nick and who I was when I was with him and before that too. Sometimes these memories come at me like a weather front, like hailstones, and there's nothing I can do about it but let them pass. I am remembering one of the nights toward the beginning, when Nick would walk me home from the bar, before he was fired, before the trouble with Cal that caused me to quit. It was about two a.m. and we were heading up Eighth Avenue. Some middle-aged guy in a business suit, rushing past us to get to the next block to catch a cab, dropped his wallet. It landed right in front of us on the sidewalk. The guy didn't even notice and kept on going. Nick scooped it up immediately, and without even opening it, you could see there was a sizable amount of cash peeking out of the seams. We stood there staring at it, and then Nick looked at me and held my gaze for a moment. Suddenly he turned away and started hollering after the guy. He chased him down, handed the property over, and then came sauntering back.

"See what you're doing to me, Katie." Nick grinned. "You're making me a better man."

He was trying so hard to impress me, acting like some solid citizen, but it seemed all wrong, because I would have kept that man's wallet. I would have taken all the cash and probably tried to use the credit cards. Who did Nick think I was, exactly? We'd been together for weeks by this point and talked all the time. I wondered if he'd even been listening to me or paying any attention. I was so crazy about Nick then, so I didn't let it bother me much. But I can still remember thinking: "This guy doesn't know me. He doesn't know me at all."

THE WORLD AT LARGE

Yes, Janis Joplin survived! We got along great or the truth is I barely saw her, but her food kept disappearing and there was the obvious evidence of her normal functioning within the litter box too, so I knew she'd been skulking around the apartment somewhere. By the end of the week, she made a few tentative appearances, eyeing me in a half-crazed fashion while hiding behind the door to your bedroom. In this way, she reminded me of the actual Janis, who I'd read had some trust issues, which led to her drinking and heroin use. It should be noted that both your cat and the tragic singer share a scruffy, somewhat-demolished appearance. At any rate, Nina, you'll notice that I didn't use all the litter, and the food supply held out, so that hundred-dollar bill you left me for emergencies is still in the envelope on top of that Kelly Ripa cookbook (don't make me ask!) in the kitchen.

But something pretty momentous *did* happen while you were away, which I really do need to tell you about. It all started when I went to the mailboxes for the final time and met one of your neighbors. He seemed like a nice and normal sixty-year-old man, except that he was wearing a black T-shirt with the words *Balls Deep* scrawled on it in wild cursive lettering. He eyed me suspiciously at first and asked if I was new to the building, so I told him I was only there to feed your cat and pick up your mail while you were away in Toronto shooting a scene or two in an independent film.

"Yes," he said in a wistful, knowing style, "the actress in four-C."

He then proceeded to mention others in the building who worked in the entertainment industry: a Tony-nominated actor, an ancient Borscht Belt comedian, and a production intern at *Good Morning America*.

"We get a lot of artist types around here, given the proximity to the Theater District and so forth," he said in a proud manner.

I didn't tell him that there were artist types scattered in all the buildings around Manhattan and probably more per capita in Brooklyn, Queens, and the Bronx. (I wasn't so sure about Staten Island.) But this got me thinking about the time I used to think of myself as an "artist type" too, which was many years ago or maybe just last week.

"So, are you a cat-sitter or an actual friend?" he asked me in a blunt, unblinking way.

I found myself telling him the truth, which is that at one time you and I had been quite close, back when we took an acting class together, but then we had drifted apart. (I didn't tell him the *sordid* details for fear it would all end up on TMZ if your fame suddenly surged!) I further explained how we had bumped into each other at the farmers market some months ago and have been trying out the friendship thing again ever since. Apparently, cat-sitting is part of this natural friend-retrieval process.

"You an actor too?" the neighbor then asked me, ungrammatically, while scrunching up his face, trying to picture me as someone relevant or recognizable.

"Nah," I told him flatly, "that ship has sailed."

I didn't mention the only theater job I was ever offered was that summer replacement gig for *Naked Boys Singing,* which I didn't take because flopping around onstage in an undressed condition would have been far tougher for me to discuss with my parents than coming out had been at the time. (However, it is distressing to realize that paid offers of public nudity, fifteen years and twenty pounds later, will not be coming around again!) I mumbled something to your neighbor about giving the *biz* up to be an events planner at the Marriott, but he had already moved on in his star-fucker way to asking some questions about you.

"She was on *SVU* a few weeks ago, wasn't she?" he asked hopefully.

I didn't tell him that a *Law and Order* credit was as obligatory to a working New York actor as fluctuating self-esteem. Instead, I answered, "Yes, she played a dominatrix strangled with a sex toy by one of her clients."

"I knew it!" he said brightly, "I thought that was her. Oh, she was very good in that. Very convincing."

He somehow managed to say this without any apparent irony or even creepiness. Then he wanted me to list some more of your credits, so I mentioned your two summers at Williamstown and your story arc on *Burn Notice* (his expression was appropriately puzzled at the mention of that old, unwatched series) and then the funny guest spots you are doing on the Netflix thing and of course (to add some prestige) your work with Shakespeare in the Park, but then I couldn't remember whether you'd actually done a show there or maybe you just had a good audition, since this was back when we weren't speaking and you had only told me about it after the fact. When your neighbor asked which production you were in, I said it was the one with a beheading and an Elizabethan dance. This sounded vague enough, but also plausible. Still, you may have to sort all this out if he ever works up the courage to speak to you himself.

Meanwhile I couldn't stop glancing at his shirt, and so I guess he felt compelled to explain.

"My son's band," he said breezily, motioning to the vulgar phrase.

"Oh," I answered, figuring this was the safest response, while remembering the amusing T-shirt people were wearing about five or twelve years ago that simply read *Some Shitty Band*. But, of course, I didn't mention this to your neighbor for fear of offending him.

"It's an alternative funk rock cover band," he clarified, though I hadn't asked. I didn't want to think too much about what kind of music this might entail, but I imagined a lot of weed smoke and small, dark venues.

"My boy, Milo, he plays bass," he further enlightened me, "and not like a guitar player plays bass, but like a bass player plays bass."

This was spoken as if it was a phrase Milo had muttered to his parents a hundred times, but had now finally sunk in, so his dad felt the need to spread it around some to relative strangers.

"He's on tour at the moment, but they don't have a tour bus, just a van that's always breaking down. My wife and I try to attend as many shows as possible, at least the ones on the Eastern Seaboard, but in March we drove to Indianapolis and saw him there too. We're just grateful he's gotten his life together. We had some rough times with our little guy. Got into some scrapes back when he was a teenager and even beyond. Kids grow up too fast in this city, but my wife and I didn't want to go the suburban route either, because we couldn't see Milo growing up in that milieu, but anyway he's turned twenty-five now and straightened himself out, so it's all good."

I realized I was going to have the word *milieu* stuck in my head for a while, as well as that overused phrase *it's all good*. I began to wonder how challenging things must have been for these parents to be grateful now that their son bums around the country as part of a band called Balls Deep in a van that is always breaking down. I couldn't help but envision desperate late-night phone calls and scores of Western Union transactions, so I felt bad for the man and his wife, who I'd begun to picture as a spunky Sally Field type. Plus, they had to spend time in Indiana in poorly lit, unventilated places listening to covers of music that had been terrible the first time around. This seemed worst of all. But perhaps naming the boy Milo to begin with had put some of this in motion.

You couldn't help but worry about Milo's parents, though, and their long-term investment of love. How exhausting it seemed, with its law of diminishing returns. This naturally started me thinking about Armando and our own issues and how he's always nattering on about the settling-down thing and having kids. He wants three of them—two boys and a girl. I glaze over when he starts in on the hypothetical names. (I think I've already told you some of this.) And since I have less than two months remaining in my thirties, I've figured it won't be long before he starts coming at me harder than usual about making some big life decisions. Armando does not want us to wait too long to start a family, because he says he declines to be one of those elderly dads at peewee soccer falling asleep in a lawn chair. He tells me I'm risk averse too, but this term also pops up when I veto an Indian restaurant or I refuse to buy sushi from the Duane Reade and not just when we discuss marriage, surrogates, or raising kids!

"The trouble with you, Oliver," Armando told me recently, "is that you can't control and plan everything in your life, the way you do all those pretentious events at the hotel."

This sounded suspiciously like something I'd read in an Anne Tyler novel once, or at least remembered from the movie version I'd seen on TV, which I watched in a time-wasting way many years ago. It was about an unhappy travel writer and the assortment of quirky people around him and how they all do their best to get along in a broken and unfair world—or something like that. Armando is always taking quotes from movies and books, and trying to shoehorn them into his own life experience. He then tosses these borrowed philosophies out here and there in a knowledgeable manner, even though his all-time favorite entertainment is *Sharknado 3: Oh Hell No!* and he's never borrowed anything from that!

At this point your neighbor fished a postcard out of the mail he'd been holding and waved it in front of my face.

"From Milo," he said, grinning. "His bandmates give him a hard time about it, but he sends us postcards from wherever he is. This one's from Toad Suck, Arkansas, believe it or not, but we also get them from the normal places too, like Omaha or Champaign, Illinois. We tape them up. They cover our refrigerator and half the wall of our kitchen."

I looked down at the card, but it just showed a standard map of Arkansas with the words *Toad Suck* stenciled in the middle of it—no weird images of toads sucking anything. A lost opportunity, I thought.

"And it's always the same message on the back," he chuckled, flipping it over for me to read the phrase: *Milo's Place in the Universe!*

I can't explain why, exactly, but I found this simple note, and your neighbor's giddy response to it, rather touching. And though I felt this man and I had finally exhausted everything we were ever going to say to each other, he fixed me with this shrewd gaze before he turned to leave the lobby. It was as if he had been reading my mind the whole time and had seen all the thoughts I'd been having about him and his wife and his complicated, bass-playing son, and Armando too and our phantom children and make-believe life, as well as my many worries for the world at large. He'd seen it all. He leaned in so close I could feel his breath on my face.

"It's all been worth it, you know," he said in the style of old-fashioned reassurance, "Milo, parenthood, everything."

He even put his hand on my shoulder before finally uttering, "Take heart."

And though this also sounded like a stock thing said in any number of books or movies, it was obvious that he truly meant it. You could see Milo's past troubles etched on the man's careworn face, but it was mixed up with an expression of joy and relief over his boy's present circumstances. It was all there, like in a collage, one that might have had a hippie title like *Love is the Answer* or something equally fey and cringeworthy.

But here's the bizarre, extraordinary part, Nina. Suddenly this man's happy little attitude was spilling over into me. It was hope, maybe (or at least hope-adjacent), and it was now swelling and bumping around inside me with nowhere to go. I won't call it an epiphany, because I don't believe in epiphanies within a real-life, human context. But it got me thinking seriously about my boyfriend's movie-stolen assessments of my cynical nature. At the same time, there were jolly familial scenes playing out in some rarely used, optimistic area of my brain. This didn't last long, but long enough for me to phone Armando at the clinic and ask him to leave work early so we could talk. He's on his way home right now.

We just might have a big announcement for you later on!

Also, don't be surprised if I revert to type by the time he walks through the door and I'll have to come up with some reasonable-sounding cover story for summoning him. A bedbug scare perhaps—as no one would ever question the seriousness of that!

But between you and me, Nina, I hope I don't puss out.

Take heart, I say!

It's funny to think how none of this would have happened if you hadn't waved me down while I was buying organic apple butter at the farmers market six months ago and then later suggested we resuscitate our lost friendship, all of which led me to your place and Janis Joplin and meeting Milo's sage-like dad this afternoon and the odd happenings of this potentially life-altering day.

This almost seems like an illustration of "the butterfly effect," which I remember you trying to explain to me once after our sense memory class back in the day—the idea that a small change in one area can result in large changes in another. At least I think that's the definition. This was before the Ashton Kutcher movie of the same name came out where they tried to simplify it even further for a dumbed-down teenage demographic. I remember that night, though. We were out on the sidewalk having just come from class, where once again you'd been praised by that bipolar, Lithuanian acting coach for your superior monologue work, an omen (it appears now) of your future success. I was struggling to understand what you were talking about with this butterfly idea because it had a physics feel to me and I'd never taken physics in my underachieving, lackadaisical Pennsylvania high school. But I didn't dare stop you or ask you to go over it again. You see, I wanted you to like me. So I just listened and never said a word.

UNLIKE SOME PEOPLE

My aunt was coming for a visit. We were about to be neighbors, in fact. It was the summer she'd been released from prison. Chloe's parole officer had found her an apartment not far from us in Inwood and a job too, answering phones at a law firm. This must have been 2005. Martha Stewart had recently come back into the world after her own little incarceration, and my boyfriend, Ian, was trying to draw some dumb parallels.

"Maybe she'll be humbled, like Martha was," he told me, "yet serene and more determined than ever, now that she's out."

"Maybe," I said.

But what did he know about it? He'd never even met my aunt.

I'd been living in New York City for about three years, since college, around the same time Chloe was sentenced. A friend of a friend had hooked me up with a job here, right after graduation, as a development officer at an exclusive private school, planning events and fundraisers, smooth-talking the alumni. We organized movie screenings and gallery openings and various black-tie affairs. I had to buy a tux for this job, which turned out *not* to be deductible. I liked the events and the schmoozing. There was a whiff of Manhattan glamour to all this that I thought I deserved. The office work, however—the mailings, the strategy sessions, navigating the outdated fundraising software—now, that was a real drag.

I'd met Ian at one of our events, where we showed a documentary about an orphanage in Tibet, directed by some pompous benefactor. Ian was one of the cater waiters working the dinner afterward. He looked very fit in his red tunic. I let myself be mesmerized by his shaved head, his flirty grin, and the dragon tattoo at the base of his good-looking neck. After I had lingered a bit too long in the kitchen with him, when I should have been out with the donors, he flicked my bow tie and whispered, in a goofy, cowboy twang, "What are you still doin' back here, son? Slummin'?" That's when I leaned in and kissed him hard on the mouth, taking us both by surprise.

I thought I'd have a hot weekend affair with Ian and then that would be that, but he had other ideas. Despite his hardy appearance and sexy swagger, he was affable and sweet and not into casual hookups. He had told me this, rather gravely, as I started to unhook his belt that first night back at his tiny apartment. I said I felt exactly the same way. I mean, was I really going to get into some stupid sex debate at that point in the evening? Ian was a little older than I was and made it clear from the beginning he was looking for a *real* relationship. We'd met in May and by the end of that summer, his sunny assurance and accommodating ways had worn me down. It felt good to use some sweeter, more optimistic area of my brain. We found an apartment together way uptown, a large, grimy one-bedroom near Fort Tryon Park. It was a jumping, noisy neighborhood. The rents were still reasonable up there then. We had a dog we'd named Demi Tasse, as if he was some sassy drag queen and not just a moody beagle mix.

Ian was obsessed with the Unicorn Tapestries at the Cloisters and said he was happy they were so close by to where he lived now. He could get a little annoying about that. He'd been to art school in Nevada, not a very good one, he explained ruefully, though bitterness from Ian was pretty rare. He'd grown up in California; his parents ran a dance school in Sausalito. He had a brother who'd studied with Dale Chihuly and actually made a living as a glassblower; there was a sister who created pottery out of dried gourds. He was from a family of *artistes*. I used to give him a hard time about that. Ian was a painter. He was working on a series of grim cityscapes, which he said reflected his angry response to the Bush administration. They were dark and smudgy things, these paintings, with harsh, jutting angles. They were mildly arresting in their offhand, political way. The first time he took me to his studio, at a warehouse in Long Island City, I was able to praise his work without having to lie too much.

We'd been living together for nearly two years when Chloe contacted me about her visit. I wasn't sure what to expect when she showed up on a Saturday morning. My first thought after I buzzed her in and met her at the door was that she looked like a nun in street clothes, with her black slacks, faded paisley blouse, and terrible Earth shoes. There was something almost demure about her now. She was getting older, of course, in her late forties, but her voice was still the same, booming and steady.

"I like it!" she said, brushing past me after a brief hug, pointing to our high ceilings and crown moldings, the nice inlaid woodwork around the fireplace. These were the only highlights of the apartment, actually.

"Lots of fun details in a prewar building like this," I said.

"We have mice too," Ian laughed. "They *also* come with the building."

He'd joined us from the kitchen.

"As long as they keep to themselves and don't eat too much, sweetie," Chloe replied.

I introduced them. I knew they'd hit it off. Everybody liked Ian.

I'd told Chloe about him when she'd phoned.

"Little Gavin, happy at last," she had said at the time. She'd always been a big one with the wisecracks.

"If you say so," I'd told her.

Now, in the apartment, my jailbird aunt and my jolly boyfriend were already having a friendly little conversation. Demi Tasse had finally stumbled out from the bedroom to investigate. He was somewhat deaf and hadn't heard the buzzer. He was nosing around Chloe's ankles, making a low keening sound, his standard greeting.

"That sounds like a dirge," Chloe said.

"Yeah, it's a mournful noise, isn't it?" Ian said. "Like 'Danny Boy' as the *Titanic* goes down."

"Ha!" Chloe laughed, and slapped him hard on the shoulder.

We went into the kitchen and sat around the table, eating the bagels Ian had gone out earlier to buy. I half expected my aunt to start in on some jokey stories about her time away, some sly reference to "the big house." Her humor had always been a little irreverent and dark, but she told us about her apartment instead—its postage-stamp square footage, its slanting, wormy floors. She liked her new job at the law firm, she said, except the office manager had the robotic personality and general demeanor of a sociopath.

The dark humor was still there, apparently, lurking around.

After we ate, we went over to Fort Tryon Park. It was a nice day in June. We all commented on the drenched blue color of the sky.

"Cerulean," Ian called it.

Well, he was the artist.

In the park, Chloe raved about the manicured gardens and spotless walkways. I was surprised she'd never been up here before.

"I was a Brooklyn girl," she said. "I never came this far uptown. It felt like the frontier to me, like a cross-country trip."

On the walk through the park, Ian told my aunt about his time in art school, his long hours at the studio, and the Bush paintings. This led to some ranting political discussion. I held back as they gossiped like teenagers hating on the same boy, their voices harmonizing in outrage. After a while, we arrived at the Cloisters, the medieval museum in the middle of the park. It was designed to look like a thirteenth-century church. Ian was excited to do his little tour. As he moved in front of us to get the tickets, Chloe motioned to him and said, "Well, your boyfriend's fucking perfect. I guess you hit the jackpot."

"Maybe *he* hit the jackpot," I said.

"Listen to you," Chloe said.

Ian took us to his favorite chapels inside the museum and showed us various collections of stained glass. He had us bend over a display of illuminated manuscripts and stand in front of a pietà he particularly admired by an unknown German artist. He spent some time reading out loud from the information cards under some porcelain statuettes. He saved the tapestries for last, telling us, eagerly, how the "hunt of the unicorn" was a common theme in Renaissance art and literature, and how the tapestries were woven in wool, metallic threads, and silk. He shared so much information with us; I thought there might be a pop quiz. I was surprised Chloe wasn't bored by all this. I certainly was. In fairness, this was my third time through the place, with my boyfriend, the accidental docent.

Afterward, when we were walking back across the park, Chloe told us how lovely the day had been. Her voice was tinged with something I couldn't identify, gratitude maybe. There was none of her blithe, mocking tone. Perhaps prison had knocked some of that out of her. It must have been difficult for her to reach out and get reacquainted. She hadn't let anyone visit her while she was up there. Three years was a long time.

"I know you've been wondering about something," Chloe said suddenly, as if she'd been reading my mind. "Stop wondering. It wasn't so bad inside. It was minimum security. I got to read. I had time to think. I wouldn't recommend the experience, but don't make too much of it."

There was an awkward silence after that as we gazed out toward the Hudson, as it shimmered conspicuously in the distance. Ian had looped his arm through my aunt's as we walked. He tried to grab ahold of me too, but the "yellow brick road" aspect of that maneuver embarrassed me. I pulled away and stuck my hands in my pockets.

"What I really want to know," Ian asked my aunt, tilting his head in my direction, "is what was this guy like growing up?"

Chloe waited a beat or two before answering.

"Gavin?" she laughed. "Oh, Gavin had his secrets."

My aunt was a blunt person. She liked to curse, tease, and lob jokes around, like some foulmouthed Auntie Mame. She had a brash, know-it-all style. I'd always just called her Chloe, as if we were buddies. Even when she was spouting dull advice or telling you stupid things about old movies, you tended to listen to her. She was a real film buff and loved to recite entire plots, start to finish. She'd been an actress when she was young, in New York, but not very successfully. I saw her perform once. I was ten years old and my parents had taken me into the city on a Saturday night. The show wasn't in a regular theater, more like a church basement. We sat on rickety folding chairs. I couldn't pinpoint my aunt. Everybody onstage was dressed up like a peasant; the women had kerchiefs tied under their chins. They wore wigs and heavy makeup. They all delivered their lines in borscht-thick Russian accents. Maybe the plot had something to do with the czar or the revolution, but how would I know? I had a decent attention span for a kid my age, which is why my parents must have chanced bringing me. My little sister, whiny and grasping even under the best of circumstances, had been left behind in New Jersey with a babysitter. Still, I was bored out of my mind. The rest of the audience was fidgety too—shifting in their chairs, clearing their throats. My father sighed deeply every four or five minutes.

After it was over, we waited around for Chloe to come out from backstage. We stood there with the other members of the audience who'd come to support their own Russian-impersonating loved ones. Now that it was finally over, these spectators were free to put on brave, happy expressions. When Chloe joined us, her face was still made up. It looked like she'd drawn apples on her cheeks.

"Sorry, folks. That was a real piece of shit, wasn't it?" she remarked loudly.

My mother, who could be very composed in public, had stiffened at the cursing. She taught at a nursery school in the suburbs and chaired the volunteer committee at church. As sisters, they'd never been close. Chloe, five years younger, had been a hell-raising teen, with biker boyfriends, school suspensions, and a couple of DUIs. The bad behavior didn't prevent her from remaining my grandparents' favorite. Chloe knew how to charm them, with her shrugging apologies and funny asides.

When Chloe had moved to the city to give acting a shot, my grandparents were quick to offer their support, because the risky whims of the theatrical world felt like a big improvement over her other harebrained schemes—which usually involved helping out some lazy boyfriend.

After my grandparents were killed in a car crash when I was five, Chloe blew through her small inheritance, thereby limiting her future options. She must have been over thirty when we saw her in that Russian show, getting a little old for unpaid church basement work. Her tart and public assessment of the production was proof enough of that. Still, it was a surprise to everybody when she gave up acting for good and took a job as a bookkeeper at an upscale restaurant in midtown where she used to waitress. The previous bookkeeper was retiring. Chloe had a facility for numbers, and the owner, a popular restaurateur, liked my aunt's brisk authority, trusted her direct, unflappable style. Her sudden respectability—she'd dumped the latest loser, opened a savings account, and cut her long, unruly hair—unnerved my mother no end, as she herself held the copyright on standard-issue appropriateness.

When I was in high school and my aunt offered to take me on a trip to Rome, my parents did not raise any objections, as they surely would have if Chloe was still painting apples on her cheeks. Growing up, we went to Cape Cod or Down the Shore in the summers, but international travel was not exactly a line item in the family budget. My mother was still teaching, and my father was an insurance underwriter at a company he despised. They were *exceedingly* cautious with their cash. So, if Chloe wanted to foot the bill and broaden my horizons in Europe, then why not? She would take my sister on a separate vacation the following spring, but to Paris instead. Shelly and I would have strangled each other if we'd been taken on the same trip.

On the plane to Rome, I'd been huffy and sarcastic, though at seventeen this was my natural state. Something shifted, though, once we got through customs and got in the taxi. As we approached the city, everything was lit up and on display, like the dioramas in a science museum. When we passed the Colosseum, massive and luminous against the dark sky, I felt a touristy jolt, a tremor of unexpected joy. Chloe grinned at me with a frank "I told you so" satisfaction. Our pensione was located across the river in the heart of the Trastevere district.

The next morning, when we went out into the winding, cobblestoned streets of the neighborhood, the scorching heat almost knocked me flat. It was mid-August. The guidebooks said it was the worst time to visit Rome, because of the sultry weather and how nearly everything was closed down for the month. Chloe must have gotten some good, off-season rates. What I mostly recall from that trip were our leisurely late dinners at outdoor cafés and how hard she tried to get me to come out to her at the time. Who knows how long she'd known about me. She'd probably caught me stealing steamy glances at various hunky Italians as they approached us on the Via Veneto, or wherever we were, those furtive head-to-crotch glimpses that had kept me in a perpetual state of arousal since the time we'd arrived.

One night, over dinner, Chloe started rambling about the plots of *Cat on a Hot Tin Roof* and *Suddenly, Last Summer*. I soon figured out why she'd chosen these titles.

"Tennessee Williams was a genius," she said in a fake casual tone, "but so much of his work was about tortured people who just weren't allowed to be themselves. Doesn't that seem ludicrous now? I mean the tortured part and the unhappiness?"

I sipped my lemonade and pretended to be very interested in my dessert menu.

"I mean, today you can be with anyone you want."

"Hmmh?" I shrugged.

"Are you listening, Gavin?"

"What?" I said, looking up from the menu.

"Jesus Christ. I'm saying it doesn't make any difference who you fuck!"

Chloe sort of slammed her fist on the table for emphasis, scattering the silverware. My aunt was glaring at me with such testy encouragement, trying to will some epiphany out of me, then and there.

"Good to know, Chloe," I said.

"Fine, then," she sighed dramatically before waving for the check.

My aunt probably figured her casual cursing and dirty observations (she liked to joke about the small endowments on the male statues we'd seen in the Villa Borghese) would disarm me, get me to disclose all my private thoughts and musings. I could tell she thought I was some neophyte who needed her wise, shopworn counsel. The truth was that I'd been sleeping with one of my soccer teammates for nearly a year. Some pining little virgin I was not. But why should I bring my aunt up to speed? Chloe's wild youth was long gone, a relic of the past.

A free ticket to Rome didn't entitle her to unrestricted access to my personal life. How smug people were when they thought they had some special knowledge of you, when they thought they knew you better than you knew yourself.

It was a few years later when I came out to my parents. I was at Rutgers then. I'd come back home for the weekend to have this conversation, which I considered a formality. I assumed they already knew on some level, but I was wrong about that part. I remember how their clipped, icy reactions stunned me into a bruised silence. My father, who had never really been a macho shithead, scowled angrily at me and put his head in his hands; my mother pursed her lips and told me she would have to "pray on it." She was an Episcopalian from suburban New Jersey, for fuck's sake, not some Southern Baptist! They didn't come around right away either. I felt betrayed and furious. I realized I should have been kinder to Chloe, the night of her needling hints in Rome. She was probably trying to give me a soft landing, predicting the response I was to get at home, something that I had misjudged.

My mother phoned me up in New Brunswick toward the end of my senior year with the big news about my aunt. Chloe had been arrested for embezzling from the restaurant. The details were sketchy. She'd apparently been having an affair with one of the assistant managers, and he was involved in the crime too. There was a lot of money taken. There would be no trial. She'd pleaded guilty. Her sentence had been handed down, five years with two suspended. The facility was in northern Connecticut.

"I don't think you should try to contact her," my mother had said.

That had not been my first thought.

"She says she doesn't want anyone to visit or write. Your aunt has always been stubborn like that. She didn't even let me know any of this before it was practically all settled."

I noticed my mother's voice had taken on a voyeuristic trill. Perhaps she felt that order had been restored to the universe, now that her sister had fallen from grace. Chloe's situation didn't upset or concern me as it might have, if I'd been a more sensitive person. I remember sort of joking about it with my friends at school, getting some laughs about my spinster aunt who was going to prison for ripping off an overpriced Manhattan eatery. I made Chloe an old maid in the telling, to sell the story more, to paint a more outrageous picture. I might as well have given her half-glasses and a frayed cardigan, when she'd been nothing like that at all.

Ian and I saw my aunt fairly often that summer after her release. She'd stop in on weekend mornings or occasionally at other times. She might come with us when we took Demi Tasse for a walk in the park. She told me she'd been out to see my parents in New Jersey, a tense visit, I gathered. Perhaps they'd hidden the silverware. And she'd been in touch with Shelly too, who was going into her fifth year (and then some) at a small liberal arts school outside Boston. My sister's intractable nature was now getting in the way of her completing basic graduation requirements.

During these visits, Chloe would fill us in on her progress "acclimating to society," as she referred to it. It was going well, she said. She liked her parole officer. My aunt was lucky in this regard, she told us, because sometimes these guys could be complete and utter assholes. Ian and I nodded when she'd told us this, as if we really knew anything about it. They were giving her some paralegal work to do at her job, in addition to the phones, which pleased her. She organized litigation binders at the reception desk, labeled exhibits. Sometimes she'd work through her lunch hour or stay late and make some overtime.

"I like putting things in order," she said. "It's good spiritual exercise."

In prison she'd started reading about Eastern philosophy, Buddhism in particular, so occasionally some quote would leak out of her.

"If a man can control his mind," she told us, "he can find the way to Enlightenment, and all wisdom and virtue will naturally come to him."

"That's interesting," Ian had responded. "We could all use a little more wisdom and virtue coming our way. Am I right?"

"Speak for yourself," I'd said.

One morning when my aunt was visiting, there was a knock on the front door. It was Skyler, who lived in the apartment above us. He'd moved in five months earlier. He charged in wearing tight shorts and a muscle shirt. He was known for his eye-popping entrances. Now he was on his way out to Fire Island but had run out of sunscreen and needed to borrow some of ours.

"The shit's so expensive at that little store in the Pines," he explained breathlessly. "I just refuse to pay it!"

He stopped ranting long enough for me to introduce Chloe.

"Hi, doll," he said, flashing his killer grin, and then he ignored her completely.

He spent more effort on Demi Tasse, scratching him behind the ears, as the dog made his low moan. Skyler wasn't used to conversing with anyone over forty and certainly not anyone as unadorned as my aunt. He might have taken more of an interest in her if he'd known she'd recently been released from prison (scandal fascinated Skyler), but I'd intentionally never filled him in on that. He worked for a famous clothing designer in Soho and was also a part-time model. He was telling us now about the week he'd had, which consisted of some circular, catty arguments with his boss and a fraught photo shoot in Quebec, where an incompetent stylist messed up somebody's eyebrows. He did have a slick and glossy appearance, enhanced by his perfect summer tan. Ian referred to this look as "laminated." Skyler thought he'd come down in the world because he was living in Inwood. He'd told us this when we introduced ourselves as his neighbors, but it was only a temporary situation because of finances, he pointed out. Too many flights to Ibiza for the weekend, he said, too many jaunts to Palm Springs for circuit parties.

"Yes, of course," we had sympathized, but Ian and I never really went anywhere other than the park.

After Ian had retrieved the sunscreen from the bathroom, Skyler managed to say thank-you, while frowning at the inferior brand and the high SPF. Then he waved goodbye to us all like a visiting dignitary. As I led him to the door, he squeezed my shoulder and stuck his tongue out at me before he left. Chloe shot me a glance.

"Glad you could meet our *fabulous* neighbor," Ian said after Skyler made his exit. "Or as I like to refer to him—*the Lowest Common Denominator*."

"Oh Christ, Ian, he's not that bad," I said.

"You only say that because he's got a mad crush on you."

"What's this?" Chloe asked.

"He saw Gavin one night in his tux, when he was going out to some fundraising event. He fell all over him. I witnessed this. It was disgusting. He told him he looked like James Bond."

"I was wearing a tux the night I met you too."

"I overlooked that fact," Ian replied.

"Oh right. My starving artist with the scruples," I said, not very pleasantly.

"Real nice," Ian said.

"Now, now, boys," Chloe said.

She sounded like a schoolmarm, which was not her usual tone.

Ian's jealousy wasn't like him at all, and I didn't know what to do about it, considering I'd been sleeping with our neighbor for months, since before the incident with the tux, actually. I'd been annoyed when Skyler had made such a fuss about my appearance in front of Ian. I'd told him as much later on. Now when I saw him next, I'd tell him to lay off the shoulder squeezes too.

I had stopped living in that sweet, optimistic area of my brain. That's the quickest explanation. Ian was the one who could see our future—some hazy blueprint version of it, at least. He was already talking to me about kids and surrogates. He said there was a lesbian basket weaver he knew who was practically offering herself up to us. He made that tired old joke about "wombs for rent." I was twenty-five and too young for any of this. Ian should have been too. And could I honestly picture us together ten or twenty years down the road? A new director of administrative planning had been hired at the school. It was clear there were major changes ahead, probably a clean sweep of the whole department. I hadn't told Ian any of this, but he would have seen it as an opportunity. He didn't like the idea of me having my hand out to rich people for a living anyway. He thought I should go back to school and do something else. "Anything!" he'd shout whenever I asked him exactly what he had in mind. Ian thought I was saving myself for better things. He thought I harbored hidden talents and that I was an all-around smarter and nicer person than I really was too. He had a lot of free-floating faith in me, Ian did.

It's not that I *liked* Skyler, but he wasn't the dolt Ian thought he was either. I admit I was susceptible to the gritty allure of his life, the zippy traveling and upscale parties. I was not immune to the appeal of hearing those gossipy stories from his time on the island either, where he'd been sharing a house that summer with a hot local weatherman and a notorious porn star, among others. Despite the trickle-down sophistication of my job, my existence had been short on glitz and excitement. I was a kid from New Jersey when it came right down to it. Sex was a big part of the equation. With Skyler, it was frenzied and combustible every single time, which was usually once or twice a week, in the early evening, when Ian had catering work or was in Queens at his studio. Things had become a little too predictable between Ian and me in that area. It was like the jokes people made about married couples. The heat was gone. Skyler, on the other hand, was one of the guys in an underwear ad on a bus shelter near my job. I made sure to pass by it every day to remind myself of our latest wild encounter. I very much liked getting lost in the reverie of that.

Ian wasn't so perfect either, despite my aunt's certified approval. I didn't like his parental tone, for instance, when he got after me about the chores, when he bitched about the laundry or told me to feed the dog. He could be braggy about his work ethic too, and his artistic dedication. He made cracks about other painters he knew who never went to their studios or produced anything at all, but still referred to themselves as artists.

"Painters paint," he'd say. "Period."

And how talented was he, anyway? Despite all those long hours in Queens and the paint he could never get out from underneath his fingernails. (There had been some complaints about this at the catering company.) He might not even make any headway as an artist, and then where would we be? What would some defeated and sulky version of Ian even look like? I was making up a lot of excuses for what I was doing that summer.

A couple of weeks after he had come to the apartment to borrow the sunscreen, Skyler and I were having sex in the park on a Thursday afternoon. I had called in sick to my job. If they were going to get rid of me, then what was the point of my slogging away? Skyler's schedule was always erratic and unpredictable, so who knew where he was supposed to be? Ian had gotten up early that day to go to Queens. He was painting up a storm just then, preparing for an upcoming studio tour. Skyler liked the risk and adventure of messing around out-of-doors, or "al fresco" as he referred to it, and in my fog of horny selfishness I was happy enough to comply.

There was a thicket of brambles not far from the Heather Garden, and if you crawled underneath them, you came out into a tiny, hidden clearing, large enough to stretch out the blanket we'd brought with us. We'd each taken a hit of Molly on our way to the park. Soon I was floating on the warm, love-the-world expansiveness I usually felt when

I took the drug. I'd been a lightweight in college and barely even drank. Ian smoked some weed now and then, but we were both basically novices in that department. Skyler had been introducing me to the joys of "pharmaceutical enhancement." This had provided a nice supplemental jolt to our encounters. That day in the park, after we'd messed around, I was another satisfied customer, in a state of postcoital bliss.

We had just climbed out of the bushes and onto the flagstone pathway, still adjusting ourselves in our shorts and wearing dopey, contented grins on our faces when we saw Chloe bearing down on us from twenty feet away. I switched into some dizzy and immediate crisis mode as she approached. I lurched forward and pulled her into a sweaty, awkward hug, peppering my aunt with greetings and explanations. The drug hadn't worn off yet. I was still rolling. It was fueling my giddy sociability. I felt that if I rambled on, if I used the right combination of words, I could deflect any suspicions, tamp them right down. Extreme self-confidence was another side effect of the drug. I blurted something to Chloe about a comp day from work and how I had run into Skyler only a few minutes before we had bumped into her, a lie that added a needless layer of complication to everything.

"How random is the universe?" I said, or something along those lines, while raising my arms up in the air.

Chloe ignored this. She didn't respond to anything else I was ladling around either. She mumbled something about a gas leak in her office building, which was *her* reason for being in the park, a story that sounded as implausible as anything I'd just come up with. The only difference was that she wasn't saying it while standing next to the person she'd just been fucking. I noticed Chloe was not looking me in the eye. She was observing Skyler's cum-stained shorts, the blanket in my hands, and our untied sneakers. We all stood around dumbly for a moment, until Skyler, who'd been silent up until then, grinned at my aunt, as if only just noticing her.

"Hi, doll," he said.

Chloe started to edge away from us after that, muttering some flat goodbyes.

As Skyler and I left the park, I felt the Molly finally wearing off, along with my chatty confidence.

"Shit, fuck, crap," I said.

Skyler was still in a happy, messed-up daze. He thought I was overreacting, which I might have expected. Even cold sober, he wasn't exactly acquainted with the concept of actions and consequences.

"Why are you so worried?" he asked. "You must think your aunt has a pretty dirty mind. Why would she know anything? We're two friends hanging out in the park."

"Don't be a moron," I told him. "She knows."

"I don't see the problem, actually," Skyler said.

"You wouldn't," I said.

*

That evening Chloe phoned to tell me she was on her way over—after she had determined Ian was still at his studio and I was alone in the apartment. I could have made up some excuse to not be home, some event I needed to attend for my job, but how long could I go on dodging her? I told her to come on by.

"I'm not going to apologize for butting into your business," Chloe told me as she walked through the door.

"Who's looking for apologies?" I said.

I didn't ask her to sit down. I figured I could maybe control the arc of this conversation if I didn't let her settle in or get too comfortable.

"And I don't want any explanations either," my aunt said.

"Fair enough, but is it okay if I ask what we're actually talking about here?"

I had thought briefly that coy denial might still be on the table.

"Screwing your upstairs neighbor," she said—a swift answer that put an end to that particular option.

Demi Tasse must have picked up on the bad energy in the room. He was pacing under our feet more urgently than usual, whining plaintively, until I had to lock him in the bathroom. On my way back to the living room, I was beginning to feel a tic of righteous indignation. Some edgy rebuttal was forming.

"Can I just say that you don't know anything about this situation?" I told my aunt. "You really don't know what my arrangement is with Ian or anything about our relationship at all."

"I've met Ian. I doubt he'd approve of you banging that grinning magazine cover in the great outdoors. But is that what you're telling me?" Chloe asked. "That Ian knows and approves?"

"I don't need to tell you a thing," I said.

But that's when I really began to talk, rattling off that list of Ian's faults and my other gripes that had been accumulating in my head. It occurred to me that maybe I'd been compiling this inventory for a moment just like this, as if I'd been eager for a debate. Chloe watched me with a glum, flickering impatience until I wound down.

"I'm not telling you to settle down with Ian," she told me. "In fact, it seems pretty clear that you shouldn't. The only thing I'm saying, the only reason why I'm here, is to suggest that you consider avoiding a bigger mess than you are already in. If you want to end your relationship, then do it. But don't do it this way. Don't hurt Ian needlessly. And he *will* be hurt, Gavin. You're better than that, unlike some people."

"I suppose I should appreciate your input, but this doesn't concern you in the slightest."

"It became my concern when I saw you stumbling around half-naked in the park, but I figured something was up when I was first introduced to . . . that Skyler person."

She waved her hand dismissively.

"Congratulations on your detective work," I said.

"Ian's obviously too in love with you to see what's going on. I hope that will give you some pause, at least."

I didn't know how to respond to that specific observation. I hadn't felt lovable for a while.

"Look," my aunt said now, "for knowledge and experience to be of any value, somebody's got to hear it."

This sounded like a line from one of the old movies Chloe used to tell me about, but I knew it was also a reference to her own life, to the embezzlement that put her away and the affair with the assistant manager who'd egged her on. It had come out that the bank account where she thought she was depositing all those stolen funds had actually been bogus. The guy had been swindling her too, along with the restaurant. The money she'd been stealing, so she could run away with him, had been earmarked for another woman entirely.

Chloe must have felt she was entitled to be tossing advice around.

"Just take a breath, Gavin," she said. "Pick a lane. Figure this out. Do no harm, for Christ's sake."

She had placed her hand on my cheek, a gesture I didn't expect.

"No one saves us but ourselves," she said finally as she moved toward the door.

I spent the rest of that evening in a state of suspended gloom. Ian came home very late that night, after I was already in bed. He took a quick shower and then crawled in with me, embracing me in one of his warm, damp hugs. I was in a stew of fussy worry after my aunt's visit. I planned to break up with Ian right then, before it got any uglier, before I left a trail of collateral damage. I turned to Ian. I held his face in my hands and nuzzled his neck, breathed in the clean, soapy smell of him—and then I lost my nerve.

I never did tell him, not about Skyler nor my doubts about our relationship. I knew Chloe wouldn't say anything either. She'd already spoken her mind. Skyler tired of me pretty quickly, as it turned out. I was like the corner drugstore for him. He liked the convenience. He might have had sex with anybody who lived downstairs. That fall when he somehow pulled his financial situation together (some rich dude was probably involved), he was true to his word and moved out of our building to a fancier address downtown. That was really the end of it. My aunt had departed the area by then too. She'd found a nicer apartment back in Brooklyn, in her old neighborhood. She'd had to get special approval from her parole officer to move. We didn't see her much before she left. When we did, she'd converse in tidy, cordial sentences, without her usual bounce.

"What's wrong with your aunt?" Ian would say. "Something seems a little off."

"Maybe she's having more trouble being out in the free world than she counted on," I said unpleasantly.

It was the following spring when Ian came home one night and explained he had developed feelings for another artist, a printmaker, who had the studio across from his at the warehouse. They hadn't even messed around yet, or so Ian said. He thought we should stop living together while he sorted this out. He was being extremely civilized and kinder than he might have been. He never mentioned, for instance, that I'd been pushing him away almost from the start. I listened to him and nodded . . . and then I completely lost my shit. I wept furiously and slammed stuff around like a betrayed housewife on a soap opera. I ripped pages out of Ian's favorite art book and told him I had always loathed his work. ("A fifth grader could do what you do!" I said.) I threatened to keep custody of Demi Tasse, who I never much liked. The dog howled in muddled sympathy as I was flailing around. If it wasn't such a noisy neighborhood, the cops might have been called. The tantrum lasted for half an hour before Ian simply walked out.

Nothing had happened the way it was supposed to. I hadn't even lost my job. There was a restructuring in my department, as I had predicted, but I'd been given a promotion, put in charge of a small staff and asked to organize some high-profile events. Later I fell in with an interesting crowd—a kind of B side version of Skyler and his pals. I was back to feeling young again after so many at-home evenings with Ian. I very much liked the after-hours clubs and dancing with my shirt off and the buzzy, winding slur of the evenings, though this, I should point out, was the start of the behavior that would get me into some trouble down the road. I did miss Ian in the beginning and afterward too, his infectious cheer and lively determination, especially when I was dating some drunk and tiresome moron. There were a few of those.

*

A couple of years ago my parents had an engagement party for my sister in New Jersey, at the family home. Shelly was in her thirties by then and had been living in Boston with her fiancé for years. I gave her credit for letting my parents do this for her, even if she did sigh ironically when anybody asked her anything about the upcoming wedding and roll her eyes at Paul, the fiancé, every two minutes. Our mother and father did not get the easy, appreciative children they might have preferred. I hadn't expected my aunt to be there, but there she was, sitting in the corner of the sunroom, with a bland expression on her face. After she'd completed her probation, she'd left New York for good, moved to the middle of Pennsylvania, where she worked at another law firm (my mother had told me this) and was back doing community theater too. I hadn't seen her since she left Inwood. We greeted each other warmly enough and I pulled up a chair next to hers. We made small talk for a while. I told her about my new job writing grants for nonprofits (arranged by my father), where I was still a trainee. I hadn't left the private school under the best of circumstances.

"It's good to learn new things," Chloe said, a little too brightly. "We must strive on with diligence."

That sounded like another Buddha quote. I wondered how her unsolicited spiritual guidance was going over in that small town in Pennsylvania. I was sure my mother had already told her about my stint in rehab, so I didn't mention that. I was sticking to bottles of water at the party, so my parents wouldn't have to wonder what I had in my glass. They'd paid for my time away, had bankrolled my recovery. For some reason, as we sat there, I wanted to remind my aunt of the night she confronted me about Skyler, and how what she'd told me hadn't really mattered, since Skyler had dumped me anyway and Ian had never found out. Ian had emerged unscathed, I wanted to say—or better than that, if you could go by what you saw on Facebook. He had married that other artist long ago, and now they ran an arts consortium in Hudson, New York. They lived in a converted barn (of course!), and there was a child or two. I didn't tell my aunt any of this. I didn't think it was necessary to say it out loud. We spoke instead of my sister and her engagement and of the party buzzing around us, until I was able to make a clean getaway.

THE DISASTER BOOK

Glen doesn't even think about going after her. For one thing, they have ordered food and someone needs to be here to pay for it. Besides, this is not the first time Eileen has stormed out of the apartment after a ludicrous argument. Glen doesn't think she has much faith in him. Though this is cause for alarm, he also finds it a little exciting. He's never had to work so hard with anyone or at anything. People have always looked up to Glen—in school, in sports, on the job. He knows he is endowed with something called "leadership quality." He has courted this reputation, built it carefully, like a log cabin, but occasionally the obligation overwhelms him, and he feels up to his neck with it. It's rather tiring to always be so dependable. He grew up under comfortable circumstances in the Midwest. His father was a wealthy meatpacking executive. Eileen resents the lack of adversity in Glen's life, the tone-deaf privilege of it. She often mentions the dissimilarity of their backgrounds—as she did earlier this evening with that crazy stuff about the *Titanic*. When she'd gotten home from work, Glen had been reading a book about shipwrecks. Books about disasters are Glen's guilty pleasure. He had told her about how roped enclosures had been set up on the ships that had rescued the survivors of the *Titanic*, and how the survivors had been split up on the decks by class, separated into first class and steerage and so forth.

"Even after all they'd been through?" Eileen had said. "Outrageous!"

After a moment she had continued.

"You do realize that you and I wouldn't have been behind the same ropes."

Glen had laughed, which was his first mistake. Trying to jolly Eileen out of whatever point she was trying to make had only made her angrier. Everything he said after that made it worse, until she had grown so irritated with him she had charged right out. This was happening more and more. Glen believes Eileen is intentionally instigating these skirmishes, doing her best to push him away. She refuses to trust his reflexive optimism and his breezy certainty. It's as if she is trying to get out in front of any future disappointment by planting land mines in a well-traveled road.

Eileen has brought up the difference in their backgrounds on numerous occasions during the six months they have lived together. She has told him that she grew up in a poor area of Pennsylvania, in a tiny house plagued by mechanical malfunction and structural problems. With its worn stucco exterior, leaky roof, and peeling gray trim, the place reminded Eileen of an old man at the end of an indifferent life. The family (it was just Eileen and her parents) didn't live far from a river, but closer still to the gelatin factory that had polluted it. The house smelled of mildew. There were cobwebs on the ceiling. She had shared many unpleasant memories of growing up there. She told Glen how the hot water heater had been broken for years and years, so as a child and teenager, she had to heat pots of water on a stove in order to take a bath—which she did every evening because she was fastidious about her own cleanliness. Her father was good-natured, but unreliable and chronically unemployed. Her mother worked as a cleaning woman for some wealthy people in Harrisburg. Eileen had few friends. Some of the kids in school (who were only slightly better off) would pass her in the hallways and say cruel things about her parents and her tumbledown home, displaying a stupid and cartoonish villainy.

Her mother was not interested in bringing her cleaning skills home with her from work, and Eileen couldn't keep up with the mess. Her parents accepted their environment without complaint and seemed to ignore it all as some might turn from a crime in the street. They tolerated the house the way that it was—with its cracked plaster, taped-up windows, and mismatched furniture. The unsorted junk mail balanced perilously on the windowsills was a source of mild amusement to them. The clutter in the house had reached reality show levels by the time Eileen had left for art school. She'd fled there, she said, as if she were deserting a battlefield.

Now it is ten years later, and she rarely sees her parents, though she tells Glen they are not unkind people and have always followed their daughter's progress in the world with warm, if somewhat distracted, support. As a result, Eileen has often felt ashamed of her flight. Glen wants to meet her mother and father. He sees himself marrying Eileen one day. There will be a visit to Iowa too, where he will show her his old playing fields and the schools he attended. His parents (he imagines) will be astonished by this moody and complicated woman with whom he has decided to share his life.

Eileen has told Glen that originally she wanted to be a portrait painter. The art school where she'd gone, on a full scholarship, was quite prestigious. Her critique sessions there bordered on the enthusiastic. But the artist's life had ultimately seemed too risky and unreliable to her. She kept imagining herself squeaking out a grown-up living sketching caricatures at amusement parks, as milling crowds jeered at her work. She transferred to a small liberal arts college near Philadelphia at the end of her sophomore year, received a marketing degree, and then moved to New York City. Eileen's old artistic ambition now feels like a book out of print. That's what she has told Glen, though she still admits to an occasional throb of regret when she attends a gallery opening or passes a particular art supply store in the East Village. Eileen works as an account manager at a small advertising firm in Soho, where she has handled some interesting brands and expanded her résumé, but her career hasn't really added up, or so she says.

They met at a memorial service for a mutual friend who had been killed in a freak accident. Glen had asked Eileen out for coffee in the vestibule of the East Side church where the memorial had taken place. They were standing in front of an old photograph of Evan, blown up to poster-size. Evan was smiling broadly, looking into the camera, while rappelling down a rock ledge. He'd died the previous month after tripping down some subway stairs. It was embarrassing to say they'd hooked up under such unhappy circumstances, so they usually told people they'd met at a wedding reception in Woodside.

When Glen first introduced Eileen to his friends, after a pickup basketball game, they were immediately unimpressed. He could see it on their faces. They found her drab and negligible. They watched their language in front of her. It was awkward all around. The friends even seemed to turn their disappointment on Glen, as if it was his duty to present them with an Instagram model. But they were only idiots he played sports with, and so their opinions didn't matter much.

"Your friends don't seem to like me," Eileen had said in a satisfied tone as she and Glen were walking away. "They treated me like a prissy aunt."

It was clear she loathed them too.

"Sure, they liked you," Glen said, but he could tell she knew he was lying. She held few illusions about herself and for this reason, perhaps, he feels very protective of her.

For the record, he thinks she is beautiful, even if she doesn't think so herself. She's like women he's seen in oil paintings, slightly aloof, with delicate features and great bones. The kind of looks you appreciate over time, an eternal loveliness. Every time they make love, he feels engulfed by her, overwhelmed to the brink of hot tears, an extraordinary and embarrassing development at this point in his life. He's nearly thirty.

Glen tells himself that all this crashing about, like the strange argument this evening, is a phase. Eileen is only testing the relationship. He imagines she's doing it the way tree lights are tested at Christmas, one bulb at a time, and this is not so bad. At least she finds it worth the effort. You have to earn trust, his father always said. Lately, Glen is trying to do just that. He's been hanging back a bit, trying to appear preoccupied, feigning nonchalance. Glen knows his ever-present good humor sometimes grates on Eileen's nerves, like static on a car radio, but he wants to appear calm, like he's not planning any sudden moves. And he's not. As a young boy, he used to watch his cousins (they lived on a horse farm near Sioux City) train very young colts, getting them used to wearing halters and saddles. It could be monotonous work. Endless circles in the paddock, tightening one notch of the girth and then another. Building a relationship, Glen believes, is not unlike this, a painstaking business. He wants to explain this to Eileen, but he is afraid she'll miss the point of the story and think he wants to control her, or worse yet—that he is comparing her to a horse!

When he saw her at Evan's memorial service, arms folded, slightly bent over, as if against a cold wind, he felt a fierce need to comfort her. It was only later that he realized this was how she often held herself, as if she viewed her existence as a rainy holiday, a disappointment, something to endure. His own life feels almost dull by comparison. The smoothness of it embarrasses him. He has to remind himself that he has a very demanding job as a controller for a major nonprofit. He's not some vapid trust fund baby.

If his father is partially responsible for Glen's good looks, his genetic gifts, then he is considerably more to blame for his son's cheerful disposition. Moodiness was not tolerated in the Swanson home, and it was scorned everywhere else. Glen's father sprinkled dinner conversation with saccharine homilies, fractured proverbs, other bits of unsolicited advice. *You never get a second chance to make a first impression. Let a smile be your umbrella.* Indeed, the business of imparting homespun wisdom was taken as seriously as a church sermon. Debate was rarely tolerated, and neither were wisecracks about faulty umbrellas.

Once, when Glen was eleven, he'd thrown his bat after striking out in a Little League practice. His father came off the stands and pulled him swiftly from the field, lecturing him in the parking lot for twenty minutes on the merits of good sportsmanship. It was explained in hushed tones that this embarrassing display had reflected poorly, not only on Glen, but on all Swansons past, present, and future. This was Glen's most daunting lesson ever. For a while after that, he imagined disapproving Swansons lurking everywhere—behind trees, in the back of closets, crawling under the bathroom stalls at school.

It wasn't really so hard to remain cheerful and easygoing. *Put your best foot forward. Laugh and the world laughs with you.* Everything fell his way—friends, grades, girls. There wasn't much to be unhappy about. Glen was, in fact, confused by grim, troubled people. They were exotic, as alarming as communists must have seemed in the 1950s, and so he avoided them. As he grew older, he dated the type of women who drew smiley faces on notes to the mailman. He surrounded himself with over-aged frat boys. For years, a friend's unexpected solemn tone, a woman's tears, reduced him to feeling like a lost sailor, craving guidance, hugging the shore. He never knew what to do in such situations. Usually, he blushed or looked to the floor. He began to suspect he had no depth.

Then he met Eileen. He was, he had to admit, feeling particularly sensitive that day because of his dead friend. At first Glen believed he was approaching Eileen out of a missionary's zeal. He would save her, bring joy to her heart. She had looked so fragile standing in front of Evan's wrenching portrait. He pursued her over the next few weeks. There was something bittersweet about this pursuit, almost melancholy, but in the end he was left with a vague desire simply to make things right. He somehow convinced her to move in with him.

Early on, when she was complaining about a deadline at work, he used one of his father's clichéd expressions in an attempt to alleviate her stress.

"It's always darkest before the dawn," he'd said.

There was a long pause.

"Are you planning to sing or something?" Eileen had finally asked. She'd raised her eyebrows at him and was clearly, unabashedly amused.

It pleased him to amuse her. His father's sayings, so pivotal to his own upbringing, didn't touch her at all. She shook them off like wet snow. In fact, she once referred to Glen's pep talks as "those inane fortune cookie slogans." It excited him the way she made everything fair game. In many ways it freed him. He'd always been somewhat afraid to laugh at his father's words of wisdom. As a grown man, when one of the phrases slipped out of him, sometimes inappropriately, at a business meeting, he'd cringe with shame. The words felt false in his mouth, but until he met Eileen he believed this was his problem, as if he were a comedian with dreadful timing. He didn't want to admit that the words themselves might lack significance in the real world.

Now with Eileen, Glen's life, for so long placid and mildly boring, seemed to suddenly transform, wash over its banks, and change direction. Her gloom, he discovered, could be luminous, provocative, and it cast wonderful shadows that spilled over him. He'd catch her watching him sometimes with such wistfulness that it tugged terribly at his heart.

It was not that Eileen was clinically depressed. She didn't weep in front of the television news or have trouble getting out of bed in the morning, but she *felt* things, really felt them, gave in to slightly irrational fits of temper. Glen found this very brave. She was challenging, sulky, as tricky as a maze, though sometimes he wondered whether she was quite ordinary in this behavior and that *he,* with his composed approach to the world, was actually the conspicuous one.

This thought did nothing to dampen his interest in her.

Her skepticism was always a surprise. For instance, they currently lived several blocks from public housing for the blind, an average ten-story apartment building. It was not uncommon to pass sightless individuals making their way around the neighborhood with canes or service dogs. Once, on their way back from Trader Joe's, Eileen stopped on the sidewalk and looked up at the structure.

"Why are the lights on in those apartments?" she asked.

"What do you mean?"

"I mean it's a blind house. Why are their lights on?"

"Maybe they have visitors."

"Almost every apartment has a light on. That's a lot of visitors."

"What are you saying, Eileen?"

"I'm saying it's strange."

"Like it's a scam? Like they aren't really blind at all?"

"I'm only saying it's impossible to get affordable apartments in this city, and I wonder what kind of screening process they go through."

"I don't know," Glen said. "But it's probably more than waving a hand in front of their faces."

"You never know."

"You should alert the media, Eileen." He laughed. "I can see the *New York Post* headline now, 'Home of the Fraudulent Blind.'"

"Joke if you want," she said. "But stranger things have happened."

Oh, the way she saw the world! He'd never been particularly suspicious of anything in his life, had happily accepted everything that came his way, like the perfect houseguest. Eileen, on the other hand, could turn a lost button at the dry cleaner into a global conspiracy, and sometimes this thrilled him, made the hairs on his arms stand up. He would, he knew, do anything for her. If only there were an earthquake, a hurricane, a tidal wave. He would prove it. But she'd find him foolish for having such thoughts, and patronizing for believing she needed to be saved and couldn't take care of herself.

Glen puts down the shipwreck book to answer the intercom. He and Eileen had ordered from different restaurants, and now both deliveries have arrived at the same time. This doesn't happen very often. When it does, they refer to it as "a daily double." Glen considers it good luck, the city dweller's version of a four-leaf clover. He buzzes the delivery guys up, pays them, takes the food, and spreads it out on the kitchen table.

Eileen hasn't been gone long, but he wishes she were back. He wants to put all this behind them and ask about her day, hear some funny stories about her bipolar boss, who is also the chief strategy officer at her firm. The man keeps a baby doll in his desk drawer, to symbolize his inner child. He's been known to brush its hair at pitch meetings, kiss its forehead. Eileen is a talented mimic and can weave a comic performance piece out of a typical day at the office, her interactions with the arrogant advertising partners and exacting clients.

Glen feels sloppy and ridiculous, but he truly misses her now.

In a few years, he tells himself, when they are settled and married and all this is behind them, they will barely remember this evening's argument. It will be dim and meaningless to them, like a scrap of conversation between strangers overheard on the street. Glen sticks his head out the apartment door and looks down the corridor to see if the elevator is in service. Is she on her way back up? No? Shit. He closes the door, returns to the table, stabs at his food—his father's voice fluttering all the while through Glen's head like an irresistible tune.

Into every life a little rain must fall. Trust in the world.

CERTAIN HEALING PROPERTIES

Jay

I wrote a real letter to Mrs. Armstrong tonight, an actual handwritten letter. I can't remember ever doing that before—for anyone. I don't even like composing emails or long texts. But given the situation, I thought it would be more persuasive. I folded the letter up and slipped it into a plain white envelope, which I sealed and addressed. When I pushed myself away from the table, I felt a true sense of accomplishment.

The table is the one major purchase Gail and I have made since the difficulties. We bought it at Home Depot, and it took me an entire Sunday afternoon to put together. It sits in our living room and takes up a lot of space. Since this is a typical New York City one-bedroom (non-luxury category), we don't have the benefit of a dining area, not even an alcove. The apartment is small but oddly affordable. It's a sublet in the heart of Hell's Kitchen, and it was like winning the lottery when we found it, which was right after Gail and I got married. When we first met, we were each living in crummy places with sketchy roommates. In a few months, when the real tenant of this apartment, a guy I know from pickup basketball games, comes back from Berlin (where his girlfriend has been in medical school), we will need to vacate. Who knows where we'll end up? That's something *else* I think about on a daily basis.

The day we bought that table, we told ourselves we'd eat all our meals at it, that it would be even better than going out. This hasn't happened because Gail has suddenly developed an aversion to it. When Gail gets home from work, we sit on the sofa and eat in front of the television, our plates balanced precariously in our laps. I've suggested we buy TV trays, but Gail dislikes those for some reason too, so we juggle bowls and dishes and often spill our food. Our sofa is badly stained, like it has done hard time in a teen rec center. When I've asked Gail if sofa stains are less offensive than TV trays, she just looks at me cross-eyed and doesn't answer.

If she did, she'd probably say, "No new purchases, Jay!"

Gail tends to stress about these things, mainly because of the embezzlement, which is always floating there between us. I was fired straightaway after a routine audit. I never denied the accusation or tried to weasel out of it.

That was nearly three months ago.

As for my letter to Mrs. Armstrong, I am counting on the passage of time and the not inconsiderable power of sentimentality to cloud her memory. I went to high school with Mrs. Armstrong's son, Hugh. In the letter I mentioned all the happy times we had at their home, a large center-entrance colonial in the only wealthy section of the Boston suburb where I grew up. But it's untrue about those happy times. We actually didn't hang out there all that much because the Armstrongs hated to have Hugh's friends in the house. It was usually off limits, like a taped-off crime scene. I used to think they weren't exactly thrilled to have Hugh there either. They were already middle-aged by the time Hugh was born, old by the time he hit high school. He was an only child—"their change-of-life baby," my mother once remarked in an uncharitable way.

Mr. Armstrong was a high-strung banker with electric white hair and a ruddy complexion. He drove a classic Mercedes convertible. His brusque wife did committee work and tended an organic herb garden. I remember their forced politeness when they saw me and my friends, how they talked to us the way lead actors address servants in old movies, with a chummy condescension. If one of them suddenly appeared, you'd automatically straighten your posture, swallow your gum, run a hand through your hair.

The summer after our junior year of high school, Hugh invited me up to his cottage in Maine for a week. I was happy to accept, as my own family never went anywhere. Despite the nice car and their fancy neighborhood, my expectations were not particularly high for the Armstrong vacation home. Hugh had said *cottage*, after all. I pictured something small and rustic; maybe there would even be an outhouse. Imagine my surprise when we arrived, and I saw that enormous shingle-style structure looming over Armstrong Point (Armstrong Point!) with its eight bedrooms, two turrets, a wraparound porch, and a boathouse made of stone. The property was perched on a beautiful glacial lake. It had taken us half a day to drive up there.

This place had apparently been in Mrs. Armstrong's family for generations and looked like a colossal cruise ship. I half expected to see uniformed summer staff scurrying about, but Hugh told me his parents didn't like to mix with the locals. Hugh brought me fishing that first day, and I caught a couple of smallmouth bass. He was patient with me about the fishing and also about showing me how to maneuver the powerboat—a thirty-one-foot Sonic. This patience I think stemmed from him being an only child with ancient parents. He was just pleased to have some real company. We swam every day, racing to a large float anchored twenty yards from shore. The water was wonderfully clear, but freezing too, even though it was the height of summer.

I don't recall many people on the lake. The shore was blanketed with pine trees. At night you could see the lights from some other properties twinkling in the manner of fireflies through the branches. The sky was crowded with stars, and I would watch them while Hugh and I stretched out on the pier or roasted marshmallows in the firepit. I remember everything felt calm and peaceful in those moments. This was not a familiar feeling, given the chaos I had at home, which mostly revolved around my parents' money concerns, as they tried to raise me and my four rowdy siblings in a three-bedroom house, where the appliances were always breaking down and the roof perpetually leaked. Our home often had the frantic, crowded energy of an after-hours club. My mother was a pediatric nurse, on the graveyard shift, and my dad worked in a factory that manufactured watch hands, taking as much overtime as he could. Given their opposite schedules and the scrambling around they always did, it was more like watching folks paired up for a relay race than an actual married couple in charge of a family.

It turned out the Armstrongs were friendlier up in Maine, closer to human. Probably they were just more relaxed up there, away from the tiring business of being who they actually were. They toasted the sunset with cocktails while sitting in their white Adirondack chairs. They talked to the chipmunks. The place worked a particular magic over them and me too. That's what I remembered tonight when I found an old travel magazine in our building's laundry room. There was a whole section devoted to vacations in Maine, or "Vacationland," as it's called. It got me thinking about that summer with the Armstrongs and about Gail and me and all we've been through.

Then I remembered that the last time I spoke to my mother she mentioned that Mr. Armstrong had died of a heart attack while waiting in line at the DMV, which sounded like a punch line to a bad joke, only it wasn't. It was something she'd heard from one of her old friends who still lives in town. The sharing of tragic news is the main theme of our conversations now, though we don't talk much. I have no desire to bring my family up to date on my latest complications. I've been pissing them off since I dropped out of BU nine years ago.

My parents left Massachusetts as soon as their kids were out of the house. A lifetime of thrift and deprivation has allowed them to retire well. They live in a development outside Phoenix with an abundance of strict rules, the kind of place that issues demerits for watering the lawn on the wrong day of the week. I lost track of Hugh when he went off to Dartmouth. Now he doesn't even live in the States anymore, but in Brussels, my mother said, where he does something for the World Bank—if you can believe that.

So, I decided to write the letter. I started off doing my best to offer proper condolences to Mrs. Armstrong for losing her husband, a man I never much liked. I apologized for losing touch with the globetrotting Hugh as well. Then I reminded Mrs. Armstrong of that week in Maine when Hugh and I were teenagers and how it was one of the best times of my youth. I gave her a brief thumbnail of my own life since high school graduation. I might have led her to believe that I'd graduated from college and not that I bolted three semesters early.

I told her the truth about being impatient to finish school, though, and how I had been anxious to start the rest of my life. I told Mrs. Armstrong that New York City is a logical destination for the impatient and that like her son, I am thirty years old. I decided not to mention how the city has a way of diminishing you, the way weather will dull the finish of a new car. But I did tell Mrs. Armstrong about the bank where I worked. I may have implied that I was a manager there and that I was still employed too. For obvious reasons, I didn't mention the recent troubles. It was best to stay positive and sound as sweet and normal as possible, so I moved on to Gail, praising my wife's down-to-earth qualities, her keen intelligence, and boasting about how pretty she is. I didn't tell her how tired Gail looks lately. I take responsibility for that too, my wife's fatigue and its impact on her appearance.

At any rate, then I finally got to it. I asked Mrs. Armstrong if there was anything I could possibly do to help her, now that Mr. Armstrong was gone and Hugh is living out of the country. I reminded her that summer is fast approaching and perhaps she needed someone to open the lake house for her, give it a thorough cleaning, put the float in the water, tune up the boat. That's when I volunteered Gail and myself. We'd be only too happy to oblige, I explained. I remembered what Hugh had said about his parents not trusting townies, so I reminded her that she wouldn't want strangers doing this kind of work. *Luckily, you already know me!* I also vouched for Gail. Getting away from New York would be the only payment we'd need, I wrote. *No other compensation necessary!*

I closed the letter by once again extending my deepest sympathy on the loss of her husband and telling her that I would be eagerly awaiting her reply. I included my email address if she was so inclined and my phone number too. I also printed my return address on the envelope very carefully in case she wanted to keep this an old-school correspondence.

Recently, I saw a therapist who told me perspective is necessary to live a happy life. His name was Doug, and he looked like an older, washed-out Ryan Reynolds. I must decide, Doug said, what exactly are the important things and what are not. I stopped going after three visits. I didn't think it was working, but I guess that perspective advice was helpful. For instance, *the stains on the sofa are not important*.

I scuff across the living room floor toward the bedroom. I'm wearing thick wool socks, blue sweatpants, and a white hooded sweatshirt. It's May and over seventy degrees inside the apartment, but I still feel cold. It's a problem I've been having. My hands, my feet, the tip of my nose, my crotch. The extremities. It's an odd thing, like I'm battling the elements within our apartment, within my own body. When I open the bedroom door, a shaft of light from behind me illuminates the bed and our dressers and makes some weird, spidery shadows on the wall. It's after midnight. I look down at Gail. She is lying on her side, turned away from me, in a T-shirt and shorts. She has taken to sleeping this way, like an exhausted marathoner. I walk over to the bed and stretch out beside her. I suppose I want to talk. I can tell she's not asleep. Lately when she comes to bed, Gail just rests. She lies awake on top of the covers. She dozes like a backpacker in a train station. Gail waits.

Since the difficulties, I feel so much sloppy, overwhelming love for my wife. I'm clumsy around Gail lately, bloated and top heavy with these feelings, a Goodyear blimp tangled in power lines. I reach over and touch my wife's thigh. Her legs are inexplicably tanned and smooth any time of year. My cold hand makes her jump a bit and she pulls away. When we first got together a little over a year ago, all I needed to do in bed was look in her direction and she'd be there, meeting me halfway. I grew used to that. Not only the sex, which was always good and hot, but the actual closeness. Men (sitcoms will tell you) are supposed to dislike the cuddly, afterward part, but that's what I miss most now. The holding each other. Since the troubles, our sex life has tapered off like snowstorms do. Since the troubles, I've taken to calculating the probability of a hand job as if I'm a meteorologist on the lookout for squalls.

"What were you doing out there?" Gail finally asks with her back still to me.

"I was writing a letter," I tell her, trying to sound casual.

"Excuse me?" she says, and so I repeat myself.

"An actual letter?" she asks.

"It's not like I have her email address."

"Whose email address?"

"Mrs. Armstrong's"

"Who is Mrs. Armstrong?!"

"Hugh Armstrong's mother. Hugh was a buddy of mine in high school. His father died, so I was writing his mother a letter of condolence."

"You've never mentioned anyone named Armstrong. Are they from Massachusetts?"

"Yes. I just told you. Hugh was a buddy of mine from high school."

"Stop saying 'buddy,'" Gail says.

Gail never used to be so irritable.

"I'm sure I've talked about them," I say.

"I'm sure you haven't. Did your *buddy* Hugh contact you?"

Suspicion is rising off Gail like steam.

"Nope. We've lost touch," I say. "He lives in Europe now. My mom told me the news."

"And when exactly did you talk to *her*?"

"Well, she told me when I called for her birthday."

Gail at last sits up and turns around to face me.

"Jay, that was months ago. And you're contacting this woman now?"

"Is there some kind of statute of limitations on offering condolences?" I say.

Gail turns on the lamp beside the bed. She rubs her face. She's flushed and pink, like a sleepy infant. Her auburn hair is a mess; a few strands are plastered to the corner of her mouth. I want to reach over and make it right, but I stay put.

"What are you up to, Jay?" she says in a whisper, or really a hiss. "You write someone you haven't seen in over ten years, someone I've never even heard of. That's nuts. Did you write her about us? Did you mention what's been going on here?"

Gail is wondering if I've written Mrs. Armstrong about the embezzlement. I don't know if she'd take this as a good sign. We rarely mention it ourselves. I suspect Gail doesn't find all this silence healthy, and that's why she sent me to the therapist in the first place. And I suppose the embezzlement happened because, as I implied to Mrs. Armstrong, I am a rather impatient person. I took advantage of some opportunities that presented themselves, and now I am facing the consequences. I regret what I did simply because I may lose Gail over it. Since the incident, it's like we're living in the mountains where the air is thin. We can't catch our breath. Gail reaches over and grabs my hand.

"Jay," she says. "Just fucking tell me."

And so that's what I try to do.

Gail

When I was a girl in Vermont, we lived near a cemetery and the saddest grave there belonged to a baby named Dean LaSalle. It was the saddest grave by far. I remember his gravestone was white marble with a small lamb carved on top, and the face of the stone read *Heaven's Newest Angel* or something awful like that. Baby Dean had died years before I was born, from crib death, my mother told me. Mrs. LaSalle was famous in our town because of this tragedy and because she visited the grave every day and decorated it on holidays, driving to the cemetery with Easter baskets or plastic Santas in the trunk of her car, crepe paper turkeys on Thanksgiving and sparklers for the Fourth of July. I don't think the grave was ever bare. Dean was her only child. My brother and I and the other kids in the neighborhood were only vaguely aware of how heartbreaking all this was, so we often raided the grave for goodies, which is not a very pleasant thing to remember.

I still sometimes catch myself wondering about Mrs. LaSalle and her all-encompassing grief, the theme of her life. I haven't come to any conclusions. She's just there sometimes, like a hit song, swirling, dancing through my head, an important reminder of what *real* heartbreak looks like. I was thinking of her only a few minutes ago, when my husband came into the bedroom with one of his plans. It seems Jay wrote a letter to the mother of a childhood friend, a recent widow he hasn't seen in years, because he wants to use her summer home for a vacation. He says the woman never uses the place. He says we need some time away. Not only is this idea horribly insensitive and brazen, it's a foolish notion. As if this long-lost person even remembers my husband or would entertain such an idea. But it's Jay's response to everything that has happened.

Jay stole from his job, but we're paying it back. Debt, I have decided, is a living thing, stalking us like a maniac in a slasher movie. We also have the rent, credit card bills, and our college loans too, along with the usual living expenses. And in a few months we need to find another place to live, but don't get me started on that. I temp during the day, mostly at law firms. I work at a bookstore in the evening. I need every shift I can get. Jay's been looking for work, but he hasn't been able to find anything. It's like he's been hollowed out by what has happened. I had him go to a therapist, to help him get back on track, but it didn't click. Jay came home from the sessions cracking stupid jokes in a dreadful, Freud-like accent, and somehow, despite everything, I couldn't help but laugh. Some of my husband's charm has remained intact.

Jay worked purchasing supplies, tracking deliveries, and running errands for an investment bank. It was a decent job, with good benefits and a year-end bonus. He'd been there a long time, since coming to the city, though when we met, he told me this was just a stepping stone. He never explained his intended trajectory for success exactly, but I didn't care. His earning potential meant less than nothing to me. It was his amazing optimism that was the attraction. He had these ideas, and it didn't bother me much that the plans were always changing; I was just glad he had them.

He'd often talk about exotic places we should go. He wanted us to visit Iceland so we could sit in some geothermal pool, a big tourist attraction near Reykjavik. We would wallow in the healing properties of its mud, he said, feel the squish of it between our toes. There was talk of spending a summer hiking the Appalachian Trail or bungee jumping all over New Zealand. He thought maybe we should chuck it all and join the Peace Corps, teach English in Mongolia. He once thought we should be gutting fish on a boat in the Bering Sea and had done all types of online research about that too. Even this bleak notion engaged me for a while.

He'd go on these long riffs about our future, and it was intoxicating. No one had ever spoken to me in this way. It was like discovering a new language. I hadn't grown up in the most optimistic manner. My parents had struggled in their lives, in financial ways and most other ways too. My father wore his disappointment in plain sight, like a garish boutonniere, while my mother stood to his side and smiled ironically at everything. When I was six, they were forced to forfeit their dairy farm (which had been in my father's family for over a century) after a bovine virus killed most of the cows. My parents sold all their possessions and moved us to an apartment in what had once been a mill town. They each found clerical work at local businesses. Our lost farm was never spoken of again.

When I met Jay, I was new to the city. I had graduated from a small college in New Hampshire. I told him I'd come here to go to film school and was waiting to see if any of my grad school applications had been accepted. I said I'd been inspired by a documentary I'd seen about disposable plastic and its alarming impact on oceans. I told Jay some other generic things I knew about filmmaking and certain facts I had in my head about the indie film scene. Jay was supportive of my film school aspirations, but we'd met while jogging around the reservoir in Central Park, and a guy will often bullshit you when the endorphins are pumping through his system. I worried that some of what he spouted at me was standard guy schmooze, but soon it was apparent that there was something different about Jay—those strange ideas that kept trilling out of him, like birdcalls, so many I was overwhelmed.

I'd always been the levelheaded type, but I married Jay after knowing him less than six weeks, in a mad rush at City Hall, shocking both our families. Sometimes I think I married him because I was tired of being a rather ordinary person. It was like being tired of a climate that never changes. This was why I came here. I had the vague notion of reinventing myself, shedding my skin. New York City is known for that. You can imagine the discarded husks piled high at the entrances to the Lincoln and Holland Tunnels, the George Washington Bridge. Jay was part of my reinvention. The guys I dated before him were never too serious. Not about me, anyway. Their interest felt fleeting, whereas Jay's attention was focused, like a heat-seeking missile, from the moment we met. He told me I was brilliant and beautiful and fascinating, and I could sometimes see these qualities reflected in his eyes. This had a seismic effect on me.

We had been married less than a year when Jay called, the day he was confronted by his bosses. I was having a stressful experience as well. I was one week into a long-term temp assignment, working for a cigar-smoking litigator, who thought nothing of editing two-line memos twenty or thirty times. He also expected me to serve him lunch on a tray and cut up his fruit in geometric shapes. This I did because my agency knew he was a retro lunatic and they were doubling my hourly rate, but it really wasn't worth it. I was daydreaming about secretly filming this moron's behavior and posting it on TikTok, when Jay phoned.

"There's been an incident," he told me.

That was the ludicrous way he began the call.

Jay gave me some hazy details, enough so I knew our lives would never be the same. I shut down my computer and picked up my purse. I called my agency and told them I was sick to my stomach (true enough) and would need to leave.

I took a subway downtown to Jay's office. I traveled on the 6 line and sat across from a pretty woman and her young daughter. They were seated sideways. The mother was braiding the girl's hair and humming a joyful tune. While I looked at them, I kept thinking about what Jay had said. "There's been an incident." Like he'd fallen down a well. Now I was going to save him.

When I got to Plimpton Capital in the Financial District, I was holding my breath and silently reciting the names of the states alphabetically, which was something I used to do in middle school whenever I was nervous. I walked through the pale blue, tastefully decorated hallways trailing a snippy administrative assistant.

I'd gotten to *Nebraska* when we reached a conference room. A door swung open and I was ushered in. Jay was there, seated at a long, oval-shaped mahogany table. His hands were folded in front of him. I looked at his hands for a long time. I might have been expecting shackles of some sort. Two men were seated, flanking Jay, one of them was a partner there and the other was the head of HR. They stood up and introduced themselves. Both seemed elderly to me, almost rickety, like they needed to be shored up with matchbooks. They pointed to a seat, but I don't remember sitting. I hadn't spoken yet. I was still too busy looking at Jay's hands.

"We have a situation, Mrs. Lyle . . . ," the HR man started. "We're sorry to bring you down here. Your husband insisted on calling you. He assured us that you knew nothing about any of this. Under normal circumstances, he should really be consulting an attorney."

I wanted to tell them I was not *Mrs.* Lyle, because I was only twenty-five and had kept my own name, but I anticipated their elderly disapproval (and the rolling of their milky eyes), so I said nothing.

"But given Jay's years here," the man went on, in the style of someone presenting a posthumous award, "and how well-liked he has been, the firm is willing to try to handle this informally."

Then they explained.

Jay had been receiving personal reimbursement for falsified office purchases. He also admitted dipping into the petty cash drawer, falsifying those records too, perhaps getting away with thousands, but they could only estimate the exact sum.

"We'll pay you back" is all I remember saying. Whenever one of these old men started to say anything, I said it again. It was like a mantra. "We'll pay you back."

I don't know how long I was there, how many times I had to say it. I know I didn't cry. At one point I could hear Jay making snuffling sounds, wiping his nose on his sleeve, but I couldn't bear to look him in the face. In the end, they drew up an agreement. It requires us to pay back a set amount every month, a figure almost as much as our rent. They reserve the right to prosecute Jay, but they said they have no plans to do so if he honors the agreement. Of course, he was terminated, without benefits, immediately. They told me how personally disappointed they both were, how they thought they knew my husband. It was like being in the principal's office. I despised their smug superiority, and for a moment I was pleased Jay had ripped them off. It was not lost on me that the partner sitting across the table was probably wearing a four-thousand-dollar suit.

When Jay and I finally left his office building that day, we began walking. We walked all the way home to Forty-Sixth Street, up through the narrow streets of the Financial District, on into Chinatown and Little Italy, past some fancy Soho shops, and then across town. It was February and freezing, and we walked fast. I set the pace, even though I'm of average height and Jay has these long legs. Maybe adrenaline had finally kicked in. Maybe I was half running. All I know is that Jay didn't try to speak. He only stayed alongside, turning occasionally to look at me.

At home, I sat on the bed with the laptop, and I made Jay bring me the checkbook and unpaid bills, show me all the balances online. Jay had always handled our finances. He'd wanted it that way, and after what it was like for me growing up, with my parents tossing a coin to decide which utility bill to pay, I was pleased to be free of the responsibility. Now I made a long list of our debts and then I began to work out a budget. Jay was already in denial. He went out for another long walk while I called our creditors and arranged as many special arrangements as I could. I registered with some other temp agencies and later found evening work at a bookstore in the neighborhood. I knew then I had signed on for the duration. I was reminded of my parents and all they'd lost, how they adjusted, supported each other, and moved on. I couldn't figure out where the money had gone, the money Jay had pilfered. According to him, the stealing had begun around the time we met, but he absolutely refused to elaborate, other than to insist it was not for opioids or a gambling habit or the result of some other secret life, which I suppose should have been a relief to me. He was so undone by what had happened; I didn't care to force the issue. The word *embezzlement* conjures specific images. We'd had a lively honeymoon in the Berkshires, but there was really nothing to suggest a grand lifestyle.

It took me a while to realize it was probably nothing more than those ridiculous dinners.

During the weeks we dated and our ten months of marriage, it was Jay's habit to meet me at my temp jobs and take me out, whisk me away several nights a week to different areas of the city. It was something I came to count on. Sometimes the restaurants had white tablecloths, soft lighting, and celebrity chefs. The waiters, occasionally, were insufferable.

Taking me out like this was Jay's way of showing off. It's where we would unwind from our respective days, where he would tell me those travel plans of his, the words settling over me like an old quilt, as he ordered expensive wine for us and whatever we wanted from the menu. I'd sit back, sometimes with my shoes discreetly off under the table, running my foot up his leg, falling in love with him, picturing our lives together. I never once questioned the expense of these meals, not once, not when the checks arrived, not when Jay produced the cash or spread the bills out across the table as if they were playing cards.

And in this way, I suppose you could say I was in on it.

After Jay was fired, we purchased a table where we could eat our meals. It was my idea, but I can't bring myself to even sit there now. It's strange, I know, but I hate that table. It reminds me of everything else. Instead, we sit on the sofa and eat ramen noodles or mac and cheese in front of the television. Old films are best to watch because they bear little resemblance to how people live in the world today. When he's not out looking for work, Jay does small projects around the apartment. The bathroom is well-grouted, the closets are organized, the laundry is washed. He tries. I'll give him that.

Jay still doesn't know that I never really applied to those film schools. The day I met him, I was showing off too, trying to catch his rhythm and hold his interest. Later it would have felt like a betrayal to tell him. I was embarrassed to admit I hadn't worked out a dream of my own, one that required graduate work or anything else. I had told him I was rejected from all the film programs. He was empathetic and held my hand, urging me to apply again. I'd like to think it was the same way I tried to encourage him whenever he talked of visiting that geothermal pool in Iceland with its certain healing properties.

I fantasize about the future. One day, when all the bills are paid and I no longer feel half-culpable for what Jay did, I will pack my things, leave a note, and close the door quietly behind me, transforming my first marriage into nothing more than a footnote. Or maybe that's not what I'll do at all. I might, instead, grab my handsome husband by his shoulders, bury my face in his neck, and whisper, "Let's begin again, Jay. Starting now. Clean slate."

THE SIMPLE PART

I had been unable to shake a depressed feeling ever since watching *National Velvet* on Turner Classic Movies. This was odd, as *National Velvet* is one old film guaranteed to make you feel reassured and comforted as you marvel at its sweet, uplifting story and admire the superior production values that MGM was cranking out in 1944. The plot revolves around a young girl named Velvet, and her obsessive love of horses. Velvet is played by the late movie star Elizabeth Taylor when she was a child, and the action is supposed to be taking place in the idyllic English countryside, except it was all shot in Hollywood, so the sets appear to have been ripped out of an elaborately designed children's pop-up book. Some people watch an old movie like this to escape the calamities of a fast-paced modern world, but I had simply stumbled upon it while waiting for Owen to pick me up on the way to his coworker's housewarming party.

I might have gotten the housewarming part wrong because it turned out Owen's coworker had lived in his upscale Manhattan apartment for over a year, and no one was arriving with any sort of useful, homey gifts. The apartment, I noticed, could have used some warming up, nonetheless. All the furniture was sleek and high-end, but there wasn't much of it. I spent most of my time there sitting on a snow-white sofa in the spacious living room. I was not, as I mentioned, in a party mood. The walls of the living room were pale and bare, except for an occasional framed photo of our host staring into the camera with a fixed intensity while standing in front of some remote tourist attraction, in places like Zanzibar or the Maldives. There were floor-to-ceiling windows in this room, looking out on the East River, and beyond that, the flickering, grim landscape of Queens, which is where Owen and I each lived, but in different neighborhoods. The host's cat was perched on a pillow on the floor, ignoring the guests and gazing out one of the enormous windows in a wistful, penitent way, perhaps remembering something from her distant past.

The cat was also sleek and beautiful, like the apartment itself, as if she had been genetically altered to go with the decor. I realized this was an uncharitable thought and attributed it to a spark I might have witnessed between Owen and our host when we arrived. They had greeted each other awkwardly, going in for a hug that didn't really land. Then Owen had made some nervous, conventional remarks about the lovely apartment without really looking at it. He took a few steps toward the huge windows and praised the river, which was barely visible in the purple twilight. He put his hand above his eyes and scanned the horizon, as if he were a sailor on the deck of a ship. I was then introduced to the host with unnerving nonchalance. Owen did not use a label to describe our relationship. He simply offered up my first name, where it hung in the air, like a dangling participle. We had not discussed a particular term to describe the status of things between us, and this was perhaps an oversight considering we were now at a party where introductions needed to be made.

Owen worked for a famous clothing designer, but on the administrative end of things, in the HR department at the flagship store. The host of the party was a stylist of some kind or something else glamour related. I'm not sure if this was ever clarified. I might have asked the host myself, but he was too busy with his party, passing trays of coconut shrimp around and otherwise doing his best (I thought) to ignore me. He was about my age, thirty-three or so, but better-looking and in better shape. I hadn't worked out for a few months, not since meeting Owen. This was not because I was perpetuating some tired cliché about how people will let themselves go after they pair up and are taken off the market. It was because my gym had literally burned down.

Most of the guests worked at the fashion house. They were also sleek and beautiful, like the cat and the furniture. I would never be described in this way. I was a lab technician on the Lower East Side. I did not possess a fashion sense and I'd put on a few pounds. I did have a bookish attractiveness that sometimes I played up. I might gesture with my reading glasses, for instance, or place my hand under my chin in a pensive way, even if I wasn't thinking about anything out of the ordinary. Some guy trying to pick me up on the subway once told me I looked like a sexy Harry Potter, a comment I considered disturbing on multiple levels. At the party, I was wearing a blue Woolrich sweater I particularly liked and some loose-fitting jeans. I felt decidedly underdressed. One of the guests was wearing an ascot. Owen was underdressed too, but he was so conventionally handsome it wouldn't have mattered if he'd shown up wearing a barrel and suspenders.

From my spot on the sofa, I watched Owen mingling, if you could call it that, in a professionally serious manner, as if conducting exit interviews. I could hear the famous fashion designer's name being whispered in reverential tones, but he was not at the party, of course, because he was in Copenhagen or Montevideo doing pointless things in the name of fashion. As I observed Owen in his interactions, I saw that most of his colleagues treated him warmly enough, but a few seemed wary, as if any misplaced word might end up in their personnel file. This seemed to be an object lesson in why one should never attend parties with people from work, or perhaps it said something else about Owen that I should be filing away for later.

I sipped some wine and thought some more about *National Velvet*. It occurred to me that my glum mood might have had something to do with Elizabeth Taylor herself. When *National Velvet* was shot, she was a sweet, bright-eyed little girl. It was hard for me to reconcile this image of her with the world-weary adult she had turned out to be. I thought of Liz prancing her horse around that fake-looking England, and then I thought of what I'd read of her eight doomed marriages. Her third marriage was the most interesting to me because it was to the theatrical impresario Mike Todd and the only one not to end in divorce. Todd's plane crashed on his way to accept an award from the Friars Club only a year into their relationship. The plane was named *Lucky Liz*, strangely enough, and Liz was supposed to be on the flight too, except she'd been sidelined with a bronchial infection. Mike Todd had told her to stay home.

I didn't have a chance to remember Liz's other husbands, because Owen interrupted my train of thought when he took a seat next to me on the sofa.

"Having fun?" he asked.

I shrugged at him and stared at the cat.

"Well, this is quite an apartment," he said, ignoring my silence and pointing at the lavish sterility around us.

I thought of my cluttered studio in Woodside and Owen's boxy one-bedroom in Astoria, where he lived with a roommate, his peculiar cousin who slept on a convertible sofa and stayed up all night playing video games.

"I haven't had the grand tour yet," I said. "I'm pacing myself, trying not to let the envy build up in my system, so I won't be overwhelmed by the time I make it to the bedroom."

"*Three* bedrooms," Owen said, "or so I've been told. Three big bedrooms with fireplaces and views of the river!"

Who would have told him that? I wondered. I considered the possibility that Owen might have been here before and was already quite familiar with the layout, including the thread count of the sheets.

"Ah," I replied instead, "thanks for telling me. No need to subject myself to all that. Now I might just have to sit here the entire time."

Owen laughed uneasily and mussed my hair like I was a wisecracking sitcom kid. I grimaced at him, as if mugging for the camera, and then patted my hair back into place. The impossible reality of luxury apartments and the random wealth of privileged New Yorkers had been a previous topic of conversation for us. We each worked around rich people. Owen had his well-heeled designers, with their summer homes in the Hamptons, and I had a collection of doctors who drove into the city from the Westchester suburbs in their red Jaguars and swaggered around like cops on the beat. I got a kick out of Owen's midwestern bewilderment at all the conspicuous consumption here (he was still in his twenties and new to the city), and he in turn enjoyed my snarky, kill-the-rich asides. We had met in line at a Starbucks commiserating over the Frappuccino prices. I might have thought this discussion of the huge, gorgeous apartment was some sideways attempt on Owen's part to bring up the idea of cohabitation, but we were clearly light-years away from that subject, especially if he didn't know how to introduce me at a party and I suspected he was banging the host.

I couldn't really imagine moving in with Owen. I hadn't been in anything serious, not since Ned. And even then. I'd also been thinking about Ned as I sat on the sofa. I had met him at a party some years back, but it was nothing like this one. It was in a spruced-up tenement building downtown with lots of wrecked furniture strewn about and bad track lighting. There was no faux housewarming theme either or fashion designers or self-possessed cats, but there were a lot of good-looking men milling about. Ned wasn't one of them. I mean, I didn't appreciate his looks right off. The first time I saw him, he was in a corner spouting his opinions at some people. He was somewhere in his thirties and had a rumpled, angry look about him, with sharp, irregular features and a rather relaxed, untoned physique that wouldn't turn any heads. Later, of course, these shallow observations would embarrass me when I remembered them. Ned was gesturing wildly that night, and this captured my attention long enough for me to notice his eyes—not their color, but how they darted about the room as he fumed. The rant was political in nature, as his rants usually were. When his glance landed on me for a moment, it felt like I'd been scorched by the sun. It was an unexpected jolt. I was done for.

A small crowd had gathered around him as he went on about how the Republicans were stonewalling Obama, screwing up his second term. He explained various health-care initiatives to us and then rattled on for a while about a labor strike in Belgium.

"This strike has barely been reported over here, but millions are affected!" he seethed.

I thought he might spit on the floor for emphasis.

Hugo, a friend of mine from the lab, wandered over. He knew the guys throwing the party, a couple of NYU professors who owned the building. Hugo watched me watching Ned.

"Not that one, sweetie," Hugo said. "That one thinks he's the smartest guy in the place."

"Well, maybe he is," I said.

I was thinking of all the Kardashian talk I'd had to wade through to get to this side of the room.

"It's not a problem that he *is* the smartest," Hugo said, "only that he'll spend half the evening telling you about it."

"No worries," I said. "I'm just a casual observer here."

"Yeah, right," he replied.

Hugo knew I didn't have a boyfriend, and he'd often heard me lament the dearth of decent, viable men in the city, a common complaint if ever there was one. It was like discussing the reliability of the subway system. I'd told Hugo I hated the dating sites that pitted you against a bunch of other poor slobs in some weird competition that was designed to see who could write the phoniest eighty-word bio or whose naked selfie was well-lit enough to oversell the goods. This was the world we lived in. Hugo eventually left me standing there, shaking his head as he walked away. When Ned wound down and moved to the makeshift bar to get himself a drink, I sidled up next to him.

"Fuck Congress," I said. "I hate what they're doing to Obama. I mean, come on, just let the man do his damn job."

This was a faint echo of what Ned had been railing about, but I didn't really know much about it. Ned took a sip of ginger ale while sizing me up. He never drank alcohol. I later learned he had been emotionally filleted by his parents' addictions. I blushed under his intense gaze. His eyes, I noticed now, were a deep, inquisitive brown. I wondered if he could tell that I hadn't exactly voted in the last election.

"Well, it's a symptom of what's wrong with this country more than anything else," Ned said, and took another sip.

"Exactly!" I said, conjuring some fake enthusiasm for whatever he meant.

That's when he smiled tolerantly and started telling me some terrifying things about the Brexit campaign. Later, we left the party together and walked rather aimlessly around Alphabet City. It was a noisy June night. Ned told me about his work as an activist, the various projects he spearheaded—the shelter for at-risk queer youth, a Brooklyn methadone clinic where he was on the board, and some grassroots programs he ran in support of low-income housing. He did a little union organizing too, on the side, he said, as if he was talking about playing bass in a Saturday garage band.

I told him I didn't know that there was any of that still going on.

"What?" he said.

"Union *organizing*."

"The unions are under attack in this country," Ned said gravely.

I could tell my ignorance was a disappointment to him. I'd lost some points as a result, and he didn't seem the type to grade on a curve. I decided to try to jolly him out of it.

"I guess I should start calling you Norma Rae."

He stared at me blankly. He didn't know anything about old movies.

So, I ended up telling him the whole plot, about how Norma Rae was a small-town southern woman, played by Sally Field, who helps organize a union in her textile mill. I acted out all the parts. I did the weepy scene where Sally tells her kids that they have different fathers and the famous climax where she climbs on top of a table, holding a placard that reads *UNION* and gets all her coworkers to shut down their machines. I climbed the stoop of a brownstone and waved a fake sign in the air, scowling around with dramatic importance. I knew I was taking a risk with this performance, clowning about movies with someone more interested in delivering dour political critiques at parties than having a good time. But when I saw a look of astonished amusement spill across Ned's face, I realized pretending to be someone more knowledgeable or politically engaged would have sunk me in the long run. Choosing to be myself had been the simple part.

Owen was saying something to me, but I had to ask him to repeat himself.

"Do you think Nicholai will be pissed off if we get out of here?"

"I don't know. Who's Nicholai?" I asked.

"Our host, you dope. Remember, I introduced you."

You didn't, I wanted to say, *not really*.

"It's still early enough to hit a movie or something," Owen said. "Or we could walk around for a while."

Owen was new enough to the city that just wandering the streets on a breezy March evening qualified as a good time.

"You sure you don't want to stay?" I asked.

"This isn't exactly my crowd," Owen quietly observed.

"And yet here we are," I said.

"I actually feel a bit out of place," he replied, motioning at our surroundings. "Don't you?"

I felt a little out of place everywhere and always had, but this seemed too deep a subject to get into on Nicholai's sofa. We stood up to leave.

I thought about Ned some more and his complicated nature. It was his job, as I understood it, to point out injustices, to shake his fist at the world. After we started going out, helping him calm down and change gears at the end of the day became a sort of goal for me. Getting a laugh out of him I considered a nice, little gift. Ned was quite a well-known figure in activist circles, as it turned out. He sat on various committees and was in demand to emcee events and fundraisers all over town because he spoke very well off-the-cuff and could galvanize a crowd. He was a frequent guest on various podcasts and been part of a roundtable discussion about opioids on public television. His journey overcoming an impoverished and abusive Florida childhood, which included being raised by periodically incarcerated, drug-addicted parents, made him a sought-after lecturer at various addiction conferences around the country too.

I was rather smitten with this public side of Ned, the celebrated survivor, the savvy policy wonk, someone maybe on the cusp of fame. Once while we were walking on a midtown sidewalk, a normal-looking, middle-aged woman came rushing up to us while pointing her finger at Ned, shouting happily that she had seen him discussing the scourge of heroin on PBS! Her unbridled enthusiasm at encountering him in the real world was weird and a little scary. What must life be like for George Clooney? I thought. We had to duck inside a restaurant to get away from her.

"My public," Ned said at the time, with just the right amount of irony.

Being paired up with Ned raised my own stock in the world, and this might have been fueling part of my infatuation, being with such a showy, mesmerizing person. I'd never done anything worthy of the spotlight. None of Ned's hardscrabble survival instincts had been necessary while I was growing up. I'd been raised in a pleasant Baltimore suburb, by hardworking parents who brought up my older brother and me under semicomfortable circumstances. They ran a curio shop near Camden Yards, selling trinkets to tourists, a business that fluctuated with the economy and the ups and downs of the Orioles season. I had worked there in the summers, flirting with the jock customers from behind the counter, something my parents chose to ignore. But when I did come out to them, later than I should have, right before I left for New York, they accepted the news with their customary flat restraint, as if we were discussing a new item on the inventory. My brother, on the other hand, was a dick about my news, though that was his go-to personality, so I didn't let it bother me much.

Because of the dull monotony of my own upbringing, I was endlessly fascinated with Ned's—how he watched his father knock over gas stations from the back seat of the family car or the time he saw his mother light her hair on fire because she'd timed her drugs all wrong, to name just a couple of examples from a long list. I very much liked listening to Ned on some podcast or watching him emcee a fundraiser, knowing that later that evening we'd be snuggled up at his place in Chelsea. Ned was more focused and enthusiastic in bed than I would have imagined too. We were quite compatible in that department. I'd been so overwhelmed the first time we got together I'd practically hyperventilated—a response that embarrassed us both.

I started going to housing protests with him and became more informed about the world than I had ever been. Ned was showing me a different side to myself. I was caught up in the fast-moving day-to-day current of his life. I felt very smug in my proximity to him and found myself in a fever of romantic optimism. I began to imagine our future together, picturing myself attending his conferences and lectures around the globe, as my role as his indispensable helpmate became clearer and more solidified. I saw us moving into a downtown loft together, where Ned's far-flung activist friends could crash whenever they landed in the city. Maybe in a few years, we'd move to some remodeled farmhouse with a big backyard. I envisioned happy children, a country kitchen, and a rescue dog or two. My imagination was nothing if not cinematic. I believed I could make all this happen simply by visualizing the precise details in my head.

One Thursday morning I had gone to the post office to apply for a passport. Ned had been invited to speak at a conference on health reform and Indigenous rights sponsored by a Māori organization in New Zealand. Nothing had been decided about my attending with him, but I was picturing that too and thought my chances were pretty good. Ned had left town the previous day for a community-builder seminar in Missouri. My phone rang as I stood in the long line. I had been thinking of New Zealand and some things I'd read on a website, about the country's black sand beaches and lava fields. When I answered the call, a woman identified herself as a colleague of Ned's. She had found my number in his phone. She was calling from Missouri, she said. She was calling to tell me that Ned had been in an accident the night before. The Lyft he was in on his way from the airport in St. Louis had been rear-ended by a truck. He had been thrown from the vehicle and killed instantly.

As Owen and I were leaving the party, he waved at Nicholai in the kitchen and mimed looking at an invisible watch to suggest we had plans elsewhere and that was why we were skipping out after less than an hour. I couldn't gauge the disappointment on Nicholai's face at this development, but he seemed like a cool customer who played his cards close to his vest. I was glad to be leaving. My silly suspicions about our host, plus those lingering thoughts of Ned, were getting in the way of my enjoying the evening. Owen must have sensed some of this. When we got out onto the street, he said, "Better?"

"What do you mean?"

"You seemed pretty miserable up there."

"Is that the real reason why we left?" I asked.

"That's not such a bad reason, is it?"

Owen put his arm around my shoulders. I was struck by the concerned note in his voice. Sometimes Owen looked at me like he knew me better than I knew myself—an alarming notion. I wasn't sure why he was even wasting his time. As we walked down First Avenue, I knew I should probably be telling him about Ned, as that relationship was already impacting us and he didn't even know it. I should give Owen the whole rundown and tell him the story of how Ned and I had met, his political rants and my Norma Rae impersonation. I should tell him how I'd fallen so hard for the guy; it was like being yanked off a cliff. I wouldn't be able to spend too much time on that. I'd have to get to the bad part pretty fast and tell him about that day in the post office when I got the news, how my legs had buckled underneath me, and how I had crashed to the floor. I'd dropped my phone in the process and broken it, so not only was I submerged in grief, but once I got my wits about me, I had to go deal with Verizon.

I had the strangest idea that the world would stop and take notice of Ned's passing, that his death would somehow be front-page news, as if he really were George Clooney. I think I expected strangers to embrace me on the street and post their condolences to Instagram. It was the actual circumstances that felt surreal. I tracked down Ned's older sister. Ned told me they had always been close, *growing up in the trenches,* as he referred to it—surviving those crazy, reeling parents. When I reached Lylah in Florida, I confirmed that she'd already heard the news. Then I found myself rambling on about how much she meant to her brother. I reminded her of a story Ned had shared on one of the podcasts about their childhood, how they'd hidden behind the shower curtain in the bathtub one night while their father was on a rampage, sky high and waving a gun around. Ned said that his sister had whispered a bedtime story in his ear to keep him calm. Lylah was the heroine of this terrible memory. After I was finished, she thanked me for telling her, but not very convincingly.

"I never got used to my brother turning our childhood suffering into a little career for himself," she said.

I had no response to that. Then she asked me who I was again.

"I'm Scott," I said. "I'm your brother's boyfriend. . . . We've been seeing each other for a while."

"I see," Lylah responded flatly.

Ned told me he'd been out to his sister since middle school and that they spoke every week. I was surprised he'd never mentioned me. I asked Lylah about the funeral arrangements. Ned's body had been flown to Tallahassee, where he was to be buried next to a grandmother who he never talked about. I wanted to know the details so I could be there, but this was when Lylah told me that the funeral service would be *family only*. Her parents, she explained, were sober and law-abiding now, but during their recovery they had embraced religion pretty hard—and so my presence, *under the circumstances*, would not be welcome. I was so flabbergasted by this conversation, coming as it did from the person I had envisioned as my future sister-in-law, that I have no memory of how we ended the call.

Everything Ned ever touched was moving on without him. I was unhinged for a while about that, adopting my role of tragic widower.

My dreams of our future together had been so vivid and indelible that in those first few weeks it felt like Ned had been taken away from me after a lifetime. I wasn't sure how to explain any of this to Owen, as we plodded back toward the subway. I wondered if these notions had somehow been triggered by my depressed feelings about Liz Taylor, or perhaps it was the other way around. That's when the idea came to me that Ned was like my own personal version of Mike Todd—Liz's third husband, the charismatic charmer who went down in the plane. Liz must have lost her mind then too. In my own blazing sorrow, I might not have immediately married Eddie Fisher, as Liz had done, but I did have a couple of Grindr hookups I wish I could take back and then I had continued to wander around in a lost, erratic state for longer than I now care to admit. I had used up all my personal time at work and had even taken a leave of absence. When I got back there, nearly everyone I encountered either expressed concern about my moody behavior or registered a formal complaint.

It was Hugo who eventually jumped in. He sat me down one morning in his office and urged me to get some help. When I dismissed that idea, he pounded his desk and told me I was making a fool of myself, because Ned and I had only been together a few months and on top of that Ned had been one of the biggest players around. He was sleeping with half the city, Hugo said. In fact, he had been sleeping with Ned himself. One time he was even in bed with him when I happened to call. I thought Ned was still at a conference in San Francisco, but he had apparently been back in town for days. Hugo told me how Ned had described a fake California sunset to me over the phone and a view of the Embarcadero outside his nonexistent hotel room window. I remembered that conversation, of course, like every other one I ever had with the guy.

"I think I'm right to tell you," Hugo said as the information sank in. "I certainly can't keep watching you shuffle around here like Sylvia Plath in a hailstorm."

At first this news only sent me spiraling further, kicking myself for my stupidity and delusions. I was furious that I would never have the chance to confront Ned—or hear any of his excuses either. I suppose the hardest part was giving up those dreams of our life together and our happy, imaginary kids. I'd somehow managed to picture the right future with the wrong person entirely. I swore off relationships after that. My trust was limping and battered. In fact, my trust didn't exist anymore. It had slipped right off the endangered species list.

Nothing really changed for years after that, until I met Owen, whose wholesome charm in Starbucks that day captivated me long enough to agree to go out with him. I told myself I could see Owen in small doses, medicinally if you will, and this would help control my expectations—the managing of expectations being the consequence after everything that had happened with Ned. The trouble was that I had never given Owen a fighting chance. I'd been pushing him away from the start. This hadn't completely occurred to me until after we'd left Nicholai's party. What was I so afraid of, anyway?

We had arrived at the entrance to the subway now. Strangers streamed by us with fixed and determined expressions on their faces, hurrying to unknown destinations. Owen still had his arm around me, pulling me close.

"So, what's up?" he said. "You still thinking about that movie?"

I'd told him a little bit about *National Velvet* on the subway ride to Manhattan, but Owen was another guy who didn't care anything about Hollywood, so I didn't think he'd been listening.

"Yeah, that's right," I said now, leaning into him, cheerful for the first time all evening. "Like I was saying, there was this pretty little girl in the English countryside, and she was just crazy about horses. . . ."

LITTLE BANDITS

Ben and Hank got to know each other because their older brothers were friends. Hank was the reckless, belligerent one, and his big, tsunami-like personality had swept Ben along. At thirteen, they'd sneak into Manhattan, taking the train from their New Jersey suburb to skateboard around the city. As they got older, they'd go to Brooklyn to buy weed in sketchy neighborhoods and get high under bridges. One time they got mugged and roughed up by a group of older kids who stole their phones and skateboards. When Ben returned home, bloody and frightened, his parents freaked out. He wasn't allowed to spend much time with Hank after that. Besides, they were in eleventh grade by then, and Ben needed to focus more on school, whereas Hank wasn't focused much on anything at all.

Now it's a few years later and Ben is home from college for the summer before his senior year. Hank has sent him a text proposing they go into the city on a Saturday afternoon, a chance to catch up. Ben doesn't have the heart to dodge this invitation, so they meet at their hometown train station for the trip to Manhattan. Standing in line at the ticket machine, Hank jokes that maybe they should fare-beat like they used to and hide from the train conductors in the bathroom, race ahead of them as they give chase. Ben smiles and nods at this, but he can tell that his old friend isn't exactly joking.

Ben has decided he will not share much about his successes at Wesleyan, or his upcoming internship at Yahoo. He avoids this because he has heard that Hank has been struggling, still living at home, and not going to school. He's lost several local jobs and was arrested following a bar fight last March where he broke a guy's jaw, for which he received probation and community service. There was a stint in rehab, and a rumor of court-ordered anger management classes as well.

When they board the train and find seats toward the back, an uncomfortable silence settles over them. Ben begins to dread the afternoon in front of him. He pulls out his phone and starts scrolling in a reflexive manner, until Hank starts talking about a famous pop singer known for his saccharine ballads and preteen fan base who was recently killed in a helicopter crash outside Rio, along with the pilot and a couple of Brazilian prostitutes.

"I hated his music," Hank rants, "but now there's no escaping him. He's everywhere, all over the news. Everybody's posting tributes on TikTok for the little douchebag. It's like his death has now legitimized the shit he used to put out. If only he'd survived, his fans would have grown up and he would have fucking disappeared in a more normal way."

Ben can't help but laugh. He's forgotten how opinionated Hank can be. In Newark, a group of Dutch tourists board the train with guidebooks in their hands. They settle across the aisle from Ben and Hank.

Almost immediately Hank is leaping up from his seat and walking over to introduce himself.

"Hank Billick," he says, extending his hand to no one in particular. "Maybe I can be of assistance."

Ben remembers how Hank had done this weird introduction thing back when they were kids too, on their first trips to the city together. It was embarrassing then as well, but sometimes they'd meet curious characters in the process—a street magician who conjured fire, an opera singer who sang an aria for them, a beautiful woman who was a hostess at a gentleman's club. The tourists smile up at Hank, thinking perhaps he is a visitor information specialist employed by the railroad. They are a fit, blond group of three men and two women, adrift in their thirties. It is impossible to determine their relationship to one another. Perhaps they are traveling siblings from an Amsterdam suburb, or work colleagues here for an alternative energy conference, or lovers paired up in various ways. One of the women explains to Hank in her cheerful, fractured English that she hopes to see the Statue of Liberty from the Staten Island Ferry.

"I've wanted to come to Manhattan since my childhood," the woman says, but when she says the word *childhood,* it sounds like *shylehood*.

Hank rattles off some complicated subway directions that seem completely inaccurate to Ben, but he decides it is better to stay out of it. He is worried Hank will latch on to these happy Dutch folks, and they'll be joining them at tourist attractions all day long. Instead, when the train reaches the dirty chaos of Penn Station, Hank sends them off with a few brief words of encouragement. Ben is relieved when the travelers vanish into the crowd, but when he's alone again with Hank, the awkwardness returns, steeps like tea. Hank suggests they head uptown. They decide to walk. Ben figures some physical activity might help, maybe distract them from the fact that the common ground they once enjoyed as kids seems to have been swallowed up by a sinkhole.

It's a muggy day in July and the narrow midtown sidewalks are teeming with out-of-towners and leftover residents who aren't lucky enough to have gotten away to the shore. Hank walks with great purpose. His physique has thickened since high school. Ben assumes there must have been some weight room privileges at the rehab. Hank's wearing cargo shorts, a muscle shirt, and a backward baseball cap over a crew cut. An angry-looking scorpion tattoo, new since the last time Ben saw him, is snaking down Hank's left forearm with some kind of cursive script above it, a Bible quotation or song lyrics perhaps, which Ben tries hard not to decipher for fear of what it might reveal. Hank's chiseled and handsome features have always been rather undercut by the slightly arrogant expression on his face and a skinhead gleam to his green eyes, the way scaffolding can screw up the beautiful facade of a building.

With his swinging, bulky arms and long strides, pedestrians coming from the other direction dodge out of Hank's way, as if avoiding a careening truck. Ben, who is a little shorter than Hank and retains the same wiry build from their skateboarding days, has trouble matching his old friend's loping motion. Every block or so, he must incorporate a skipping maneuver to keep up with him. As they reach Columbus Circle, Hank slows down and begins pointing out favorite skate spots from their past, certain areas where they'd ollied or landed 50-50s or wiped out. They pass Lincoln Center, and Ben remembers how, in their skateboarding days, when they were spotted anywhere in this vicinity, whistles would blow, and a phalanx of uniformed security guards would suddenly materialize to run them off.

"I loved all that shit," Hank says dreamily, as if reading Ben's mind. "I loved the chase. We were such little badasses back then, such little bandits."

He turns to Ben and fixes him with that skinhead gleam.

"Yep, those were the days," Ben responds, though he winces a bit when this geriatric phrase slips from his mouth.

Hank doesn't appear to be listening.

"Remember those girls we hooked up with that time?" he's asking now as they make their way up Broadway amid the thump of noisy traffic.

"What girls?"

"Two older girls. We were like fourteen or fifteen. We met them at Bethesda Fountain. They took us behind the bandshell."

"Bro, that did not happen," Ben responds.

"Fuck yeah, it happened."

"I'd remember hooking up behind the bandshell when I was fourteen," says Ben. "We met girls sometimes, but the physical stuff was later on for me."

"You mean with Lydia?" Hank says, smirking.

"It doesn't matter. I just know it wasn't with some random girl in the park."

"Jesus, man, don't get so offended. Maybe you've blocked it out or something because it insults the memory of your *perfect relationship* with your ex-girlfriend, but it's not like you two are still together."

"I know that," Ben says, "but I'm not blocking anything out either."

Ben hasn't seen Lydia since they broke up shortly after high school graduation. Despite what Hank has implied about the relationship, it was far from perfect. They hadn't even slept together. Ben remembers the relationship as one long, frustrating slog, like watching a foreign film without the benefit of subtitles. He assumed they had paired up because they had compatible temperaments and looked very cute together. These facts tended to generate the goodwill of others. The fawning approval of their families and friends kept them together for longer than it should have.

Lydia had often expressed a singular distaste for Hank.

She'd once asked him, "Is Hank, like, *undiagnosed* or what? Something is definitely off with that guy."

"Who's to say?" Ben had told her.

It occurs to Ben that they haven't discussed any specific plan for this afternoon. Hank may want to keep walking like this, reminiscing about their past or making shit up, all the way to the tip of Manhattan. But when they approach a popular burger joint on the Upper West Side, Hank shoots his hand up like a crossing guard.

"I'm fucking hungry, man," he says.

Hank suggests they grab some burgers and walk to Central Park and eat there. Ben is sweaty and wrung out from the long walk. He'd prefer to sit inside with the air-conditioning, but he knows from experience it is simply easier to agree with Hank. Besides, the place is a mob scene. They'd never get a table. The greasy burgers and high-caloric shakes are famous in the city, but they hardly justify the crazy Disney World crowds.

As they stand in the unfathomably long line, Hank turns around to the middle-aged woman behind him and in a too-loud voice asks her where she's from and what brings her to the city. Ben groans and says "Ahh, crap" under his breath.

The woman is checking her phone. She looks up.

"I'm from right here," she remarks coolly.

"Here?"

"New York."

"But originally?" Hank says, blundering on.

The woman blinks and pauses, then she answers even more icily, "That would be Cincinnati."

Hank smiles and tilts his head at her in a clueless way. Something is about to happen, and suddenly Ben knows exactly what it is. Hank thrusts out his hand and introduces himself.

"Hank Billick," he bellows.

Unlike the Dutch tourists, this woman wants none of it. Something in her shrinks back, though her tone is forceful enough when she responds.

"Nope. This isn't happening," she says, waving her hand in the air.

"Excuse me?" Hank says.

"Whatever *this* is," she answers, motioning at the empty space between them. "I'm not going to greet you or answer any more of your questions. Okay?"

Hank still has his hand out, floating in midair, as if it's a prosthetic limb, a prop he has no control over.

At this point, Ben feels driven to diplomacy.

"I'm so sorry," he tells the woman. "My buddy can be a little overeager."

He slaps Hank's muscular shoulder. He laughs for emphasis. "He's like a big golden retriever sometimes, only wanting to be friendly. It's nothing to worry about."

Ben's voice sounds hollow and forced, even to him.

The woman gazes crossly at Ben. It's obvious that his credibility has been compromised by his own proximity to Hank—and his breezy mansplaining probably hasn't helped matters either.

"I'm not in the least bit worried," the woman says. "I simply don't appreciate the intrusion. I'm here to get my lunch and not make any new friends. Try explaining *that* to your buddy."

Hank has finally put his hand down. His mouth is slack and his ears are very pink.

A few beats later he turns to Ben.

"What the fuck was that about?" he hisses.

Ben offers a noncommittal shrug and a benign expression, hoping to avoid the postmortem. Mercifully the line begins to lurch forward. They give their orders to a teenager in a hairnet. Hank's voice is sharp and aggressive when he asks for a cheeseburger, but the kid is unfazed, probably because he's used to facing a variety of high-maintenance New Yorkers. They pay for the food and the cashier hands Ben a small disk that looks like a hockey puck, the kind that will buzz and light up when their food is ready. They go to a staging area, which for some reason has clouds and rainbows stenciled on the walls. They linger here waiting for the food, standing as far away from the angry woman as possible. Hank's mouth is twitching. He's clearing his throat in a theatrical way.

"So, I'm a lapdog?" Hank says, gritting his teeth.

"Huh?"

"What you said back there. What the fuck, Benny?"

"I was only trying to defuse the situation."

"You didn't need to defuse shit," Hank says, jutting his jaw out. "I was only offering my hand to the woman. I wasn't hitting on her."

Hank says this in an extremely loud tone, straining his neck, trying to direct the comment to the woman herself, though she is now lost somewhere in the hungry crowd.

"I know, Hank, but it's not a newsflash that women don't like strange guys getting up in their faces. You can't blame her."

"I was only being friendly!" Hank snaps. "And *not* friendly like a fucking dog, but like a normal human moving around in the world!"

"Okay, okay," Ben says, keeping his voice soft, hoping to shut this down.

But if anything, this only seems to get Hank more riled. In this moment he looks almost electrified. Ben assumes those anger management classes didn't take. The other customers closest to them collectively draw back and step aside, as if they have stumbled into a dodgeball game.

Hank continues ranting. He tells Ben he was only trying to be himself, but when people tell you to "be yourself" that it's the biggest bullshit of all time.

"What they really mean," Hank says, "is that you should try to be someone else entirely." Hank's clearly not talking about the incident with the woman anymore.

"You're always being tested in this life," he goes on. "You go into a bar, for instance, and some drunk bumps into you and then you mouth off, and he takes a swing. Then the shit goes down. Maybe you *do* break the guy's jaw—because you're defending yourself and maybe because you're a little drunk yourself. But it's not like I had walked into that place with 'deliberate malice,' as that dick prosecutor said."

Ben stays quiet. He stands there blinking at the incongruous rainbows all over the wall. He pictures himself floating on the poorly drawn clouds.

"Suddenly you're just screwed," Hank chatters on. "It's irreversible and further proof to everyone of your basic shittiness."

Hank barks out a sound after this, like he's swallowing water, as if he's going down for the last time. Ben's not sure what to say. It's a lot to process.

"What about you, Benny?" Hank asks now. "What keeps you up at night?"

"Hell, I don't know, Hank." Ben smiles tightly. "All I'm giving thought to right now are my upcoming cheese fries."

Then, as if on cue, the disc comes alive in Ben's hand, buzzing and flashing red. They pick up their orders and work their way toward the exit through the crowd, which parts quickly for Hank, whose big arms are swinging again. By the door, there's a smug-looking banker type in a Credit Suisse T-shirt who doesn't move fast enough, and so Hank has to squint him down and say "What the fuck are you looking at?" before they can squeeze past the guy and get back out into the wet heat of the afternoon.

They walk toward the park, past the Museum of Natural History.

"Aren't you the glib motherfucker?" Hank says in a cold, ominous voice.

"Now what?" Ben says.

He's surprised that Hank knows the word *glib*.

"That *cheese fries* comment," Hank says. "I was talking to you serious, wanting a serious answer. I don't remember you being so fake or whatever this is."

"Well, bro," Ben says. "I don't remember you being quite so pissed off, so maybe we're even."

They walk on in silence for a while until Ben asks Hank if they should just end the day, then and there.

"I'm not even sure why you wanted us to get together," Ben says.

"Shit, I don't know," Hank says. "I heard you were home from school. We used to have a lot of fun. We were tight back then. I wanted to see you and so I shot you a text. No big mystery."

"I'm not sure how tight we really were," Ben says. "We were kids. It felt accidental. Like we started hanging out because we were in the right place at the right time."

"That's a bullshit comment," Hank says. "How does anybody get to know anybody else in this world unless they are in the right place at the right time? That's the story of a million years."

Ben doesn't have a response to that. He watches the tour buses in front of the museum, their passengers getting on and off in the stifling heat. Ben reflects on the strange afternoon, the weirdest part being Hank's ruminations on life and friendship. And he's not finished yet, because the next thing he says is that he could have slept with Lydia. The statement feels as blunt as a blow to the face. They are at the entrance to the park, and Ben stops short. A bunch of irritable people dodge around him.

"You what?" Ben says to Hank's brawny back.

"Yep, it's true," Hank says over his shoulder.

Then, as they cross into the park, he begins to tell Ben all about it. It was the summer after high school graduation, Hank says, one of the weeks when Ben was up at the lake with his family. Lydia was going door to door in town that summer, working for some environmental group, and she came by Hank's house looking to get a donation. Nobody else was home, and Hank had invited her in and she sat on the sofa in a short pink skirt that she kept adjusting in a distracting way. They talked for a while about her plans to go to college in California.

"It was so obvious, man," Hank says. "She wanted something to happen. I think it was always a possibility. Even when the three of us hung out together, she used to stare at me behind your back, like in this naked way, as if she thought she really understood me or something."

"I don't care to hear anything about this," Ben says—and he means it.

"But the point is, I wouldn't do it," Hank tells him.

He tells Ben he couldn't betray him in this way, even though they had stopped hanging out by then and Ben's parents were telling everybody in town what a bad influence he was. It didn't matter. He wasn't going to mess around with Lydia, and she must have gotten the message that day, but she kept sitting there on the sofa until Hank's mother had come home and given her a homicidal look, and then she had finally gotten up and walked out.

"Look," Hank says now, "not screwing your girlfriend should count for something. Don't you think? I mean, no one gives me much credit for being a basically decent person, but in the basic decency ways, I'm a prince."

Ben can't imagine how Hank expects him to react to this nattering confession, but unlike the stuff about the girls in the park, this story sounds entirely plausible. Ben remembers Lydia had come over and broken up with him ten minutes after he had returned from the lake that summer. Then it occurs to Ben that maybe Hank and Lydia really *did* hook up that day and other times too. It would explain a lot. Hank might only be telling this edited, sanitized version to prove some shadowy point about himself.

Ben's head is swimming, from either the heat or Hank's revelations. Probably there are always people in your life who turn up periodically to wreak havoc, the way malaria lies dormant in your body between flare-ups. Ben and Hank hike some more, heading down a crude, rock-strewn path. Hank's movements remain determined and automatic. Ben assumes he has forgotten about the bags of food in their hands and the plan to find a place to sit and eat. It occurs to Ben that Hank might really be unbalanced and is simply hunting for a secluded spot to harm his old friend, more evidence of the odd and perilous nature of the universe. But eventually something in Ben switches off as he follows Hank in the style of years before, with that familiar sense of anticipation and a hum of excitement. They keep going, deeper and deeper into the park, as birds fly above them unnoticed—a charm of finches making slow, wide circles in the sky.

THE LOST OBJECT EXERCISE

Joe and I were on the roof deck of the beach house trying to make out some skywriting in the distance. It was an ad for a casino, but some of the letters were reversed. We made a few jokes about dyslexic pilots and then Joe volunteered some things he knew about the skywriting process—how the smoke is made from very watery oil injected into a heater and how sometimes the plane has to fly upside down. I wondered if any of the jokes or Joe's facts would be decent subjects for dinner. We were told it would be family style tonight, with everyone pitching in to make the meal and then we would all have to sit down and eat together. I didn't want there to be any long silences.

We'd been invited to Fire Island for the weekend and had arrived that morning, feeling geriatric and irrelevant on a ferry boat filled with half-dressed, beautiful young men. Henry List, the art historian and Joe's second cousin, had been renting a house in the Pines for many summers, a stunning three-story structure with walls of glass facing the ocean and a pool the size of a small pond. It was a last-minute invitation for us. I assumed somebody else had backed out. Joe and Henry got on well enough (everybody loved my husband), but we'd never been invited out to the island before, and we rarely saw Henry under any circumstances. Joe and I were the only couple. The other guests were single, older men, friends of Henry's. He knew them from AA. Henry was a recovering alcoholic with over twenty years sober. They were all in Cherry Grove now, attending a twelve-step meeting, while Joe and I were lounging on the roof.

We'd been introduced to the others that morning, when we arrived at the house. Alan was a freelance food stylist who lived near Fort Tryon Park. Gerald was a masseur with a celebrity clientele. The third man was named Martin Macduff, and I had hustled and robbed him thirty-four years earlier, when I was twenty-two years old.

Thankfully, there was no click of recognition when Martin shook my hand. I had gained thirty pounds since then and grown a thick beard, which was now mostly gray. I didn't turn heads on the street anymore (those days were long gone), but occasionally someone from the hotel where I worked planning events would refer to me as distinguished-looking, a compliment I particularly despised, given my glossy, attention-pulling youth.

So, Martin hadn't placed me, but I knew him immediately. Henry, during the hasty introductions, had told us that he managed a famous bookstore in the Village. This is what Martin had been doing back when I first met him. Plus, I remembered his name. Martin Macduff. Macduff was the character who killed Macbeth, the pivotal antagonist in the play, the moral center to the whole thing. Martin had told me all this the night we met. Since I didn't have much of an education (I'd barely graduated from a crappy college in Ohio) and because I had zero interest in Shakespeare, it was pointless to pretend familiarity with the information. It was easier to hang on to Martin's every word and fix him with an appreciative gaze as he improved my knowledge. This, I figured, was the best chance to keep him interested that night, though my looks had probably already sealed the deal.

Martin might have thought I was more literate than I was, because we'd met in a bookstore, though I'd really only stepped in to get out of the cold. I remember it was a few days before Christmas and the store bustled with a combination of good cheer and gift-giving panic. Tess, my roommate, a crazy, egotistical actress I'd known from that crappy college, had booked a long-term gig doing theatrical murder mysteries on cruise ships. She had sublet our apartment out from underneath me that afternoon. We'd had a scorching scene about it, and now my bags were stashed in a storage locker at Port Authority. I had no place to stay that night and had about sixty dollars in my pocket. I didn't have a job anymore either. I'd been fired the previous week. The answering service where I worked had let me go because they didn't like my phone manner, which had been described as "terse." I'd asked for a second chance, but not very pleasantly, and so they'd still given me the boot.

I was weighing my options when Martin approached. I was standing in front of a large display of books featuring the works of Edith Wharton. The expression on my face must have looked curious, because Martin sidled up next to me and began giving me a brief rundown of the author's career, her high-society lineage and Paris salon. I noticed he was skinny as a pipe cleaner and balding, adrift somewhere in his thirties. Normally I wouldn't have acknowledged him at all. I'd only been in the city a few months, but long enough to be aware of my enviable place in the gay pecking order—given my youth and surfer boy looks. In other words, I was a little jerk.

Actually, I didn't know as much as I thought I did. When I'd arrived in New York to live with Tess (a roommate had bailed on her and she'd summoned me from my home in Pennsylvania), she'd told me that a guy like me might do well for himself in the city if I played my cards right. I didn't exactly know what she was telling me, other than that good looks tended to open doors. That part I already knew. There were examples of this everywhere. Just recently one of the other operators at the service, a genial, beefcake type, had met some promising director at a casting call, and now they were living together. This guy had walked into a room, read for a part, and then his life had changed. I'm not sure if the same sense of opportunity was dancing around in my head when skinny Martin came up to me in the bookstore, but I was aware of a kind of internal adjustment. I looked into Martin's eyes and smiled broadly as he spoke. I had large, bright teeth, in the style of the Osmonds or the Kennedys. People either liked my grin or else they were reminded of Mormon fanaticism and family tragedy. I could see that Martin fell into the former category. I noticed the spark of genuine interest in his face as he spewed out more random details about *The Age of Innocence* and *Ethan Frome*. It wasn't so difficult, feigning concentration and grinning like a lunatic, to finagle a dinner invitation out of him. His shift was ending soon and he wondered if I might like to continue our conversation across the street at the Leaning Tower of Pizza.

"That would be smashing," I said pretentiously, as if I were some smiling British tourist.

As I waited around for Martin to finish up, I thought I might even ladle in a slight accent over dinner. Tess would sometimes adopt an accent and pretend she was someone else for an entire day as she made her way around the city or waited on customers at a fifties-themed diner where she used to work, taking orders in a poodle skirt.

"I like to take a break from myself every once in a while," she would tell me, explaining these invented personas, "and it's good training too."

Tess had done a year at the Neighborhood Playhouse (it was rolling admission), but she hadn't made the cut or been asked back for serious study after that. I'd seen her do some accents on the stage too (a few showcases in church basements), but her dialect work was usually all over the map, a mulligan stew of hard consonants and flat vowels. I decided against changing my vocal patterns that night, because I probably couldn't have done any better than that.

I remember we left the bookstore and walked across the street to the small, lively restaurant, where the staff all seemed to know Martin. They greeted him with practiced delight as we were led to a table in the back. I wondered, cynically, how many other confused-looking young customers he'd brought over here after his shifts. I even made a joke about that, which Martin didn't seem to appreciate. He blushed and blinked rapidly. I'd either struck a nerve, or maybe my predatory suspicions had been all wrong.

"They know me here," Martin then said, unnecessarily, as the waiter came over with a bottle of wine, before we'd even opened our menus.

"I don't drink," I told him apologetically, when he tried to pour me a glass.

"Not at all?" Martin asked, looking surprised and slightly crestfallen.

"Nope," I said. "I've never really liked the taste or how it makes me feel."

It was easier to say this than get into a discussion of my home life, where my father's drunkenness had the impact and consequences of a blowtorch. I'd witnessed enough lurching calamity growing up (my dad's lost jobs, his blackouts, my mother's zombielike stoicism) not to gamble with my own predispositions. I refused to touch the stuff. In college, I was the only guy drinking soda at keg parties. But I certainly wasn't going to share all that with a stranger trying to get in my pants. In fact, I hadn't even given Martin my real name.

"I'm Caleb," I'd told him before we left the bookstore.

"Lovely to meet you, Caleb. I'm Martin Macduff."

Caleb was a name I'd always liked, so biblical and forthright. I guess introducing myself like that suggests I already had some strategy for deception laid out for the evening, but it's difficult to remember my precise thoughts and motivations. At the restaurant, Martin poured some wine for himself and gave the waiter our orders. Then he told me about his favorite authors. I remember he especially admired Sinclair Lewis, thinking he was underrated. That might have been true, as I hadn't even heard of him. The waiter came back to fuss over us and then backed away deferentially, as if Martin were some visiting dignitary and not just a glorified clerk from across the street. This must have been when Martin brought up the business about Macduff. I don't recall the exact chronology of our conversation over dinner. At some point, though, he got around to asking a few questions about me. He watched me with such hungry anticipation. Maybe that's what put some of the fabrication in motion. He was giving me such indulgent, hopeful smiles. I told him I was from California, a place I'd never even been. I told him my family was sort of in the movie business. My father worked for MGM as an accountant, I said, and my mother had been a contract player at the studio before she retired to have me. I described a sunny, frolicking childhood near the ocean. I'd made all this up. I figured it might charm him if I appeared accidentally glamorous.

In reality, at that moment, my father was probably passed out on the sofa in the house my parents rented outside Harrisburg, with my long-suffering mother shuffling gloomily through the rooms after attending evening Mass. It was a familiar scene I remembered from growing up and beyond. I had moved back home for a while after college. I'd been working in a hardware store in the neighborhood with no real plans for my future. I'd been an indifferent, listless student and didn't have a well of ambition to draw from either. I didn't know what I was going to do, until Tess had tracked me down and told me she needed a roommate in New York. When Martin asked me specifically what had brought me to the city, I couldn't explain that mixture of escape and reinvention, so I told him I planned to be an actor, stealing details from Tess's personal narrative, including her acting school and prickly determination.

"Following in your mom's footsteps," Martin said, and it took me a second to realize he was referring to my fake mother's Hollywood past.

"Yes," I stammered, "but I see myself more on the stage."

"Well, you're good-looking enough for show business," Martin said, as he poured himself more wine. He was blushing again too.

"Oh, thanks," I responded, lowering my eyes in modesty.

I did keep one thing from my real life. I told him about my work at the answering service, though I didn't mention I'd been fired. There was a tiny bit of allure attached to this job, because there were some celebrities on the service and others who called in to leave messages.

I'd spoken to Faye Dunaway once and Al Pacino. I told Martin this and he seemed impressed.

The waiter brought a second bottle of wine, and Martin ordered us banana pudding for dessert, which arrived in thimble-sized cups. Then Martin asked about my acting classes, and so I mentioned the Lost Object Exercise, something Tess had recently explained to me. You had to pretend you'd misplaced the most precious object you ever owned, and then go about conveying the emotion you were feeling, without uttering a single sound. When Martin nodded his thoughtful approval at this, I went on. I made up a story about performing a scene from *Equus* for my audition technique class while stark naked. Tess told me this had actually happened. One of her classmates, a hunky flirt, had flexed and posed his way through a long monologue, as everyone either gaped or looked away. I knew this was a teasing and manipulative detail to wave in front of Martin. His eyes widened and his whole head flushed pink. He was quite drunk by then.

After the meal was finished, Martin paid the check, leaving an enormous tip, which explained his popularity with the staff. Then he suggested we go back to his place.

"Do me the honor," he said, rather desperately, I thought.

This was obviously what I'd been after, but still I deliberated. I hadn't been in the city long enough to make any real friends, so there was no one I could crash with even for a night or two, and those new tenants, the ones subletting, had already moved into Tess's apartment. I refused to call home or head back to Pennsylvania. My father had been furious that I'd moved out because he'd been counting on my rent payment. He'd probably already found a boarder, some lost soul, as he'd done while I was away at college. What other options did I have on this particular night?

"Sure," I told Martin. "Let's go."

✳

Joe stood up from his Adirondack chair and walked to the edge of the roof deck, where he let out a low whistle. I got up and joined him. There were a dozen or so hot, young guys from the house next door, lolling by the pool in their Speedos. We had a bird's-eye view.

"Welcome to the candy store," Joe said, trying to amuse me, one of his familiar habits.

His leering comment was harmless enough, given that we were now a long-married suburban couple in our fifties with a grown daughter. Ellie was in Italy, doing graduate work in art restoration at the Uffizi. (A friend of Joe's sister had been our surrogate.) And Henry, in fact, had been helpful with our daughter's grad school applications.

We watched the boys in the other house—wistfully, I suppose. Joe was never the philandering type, but I'd had a risky affair once, with one of the "straight" dads at Ellie's elementary school. Our kids were in different grades and didn't really know each other, so it wasn't as sordid as it might have been, but it was sordid enough. This man pursued me so urgently and with such abandon it took my breath away. It would crush Joe to know anything about this, even though it has been over and done with for fifteen years. I'd never told Joe about what happened with Martin either. It would have made a difference to him. Joe tended to believe people were moral and upright until he'd been presented with incontrovertible evidence to the contrary. He'd been giving me the benefit of the doubt ever since we met. I used to wonder if his moral certitude (along with my suburban boredom and male vanity) was one of the things that pushed me into that long-ago affair, but that's probably too complicated to really decipher at this late date, and not fair to Joe, who has always loved me in his knee-jerk, unconditional way.

As we left the restaurant, Martin and I braced ourselves against a swirling, icy wind. It had turned bitter cold since we'd been inside. This might have sobered Martin up some. His voice was less slurry anyway as we began to walk toward his apartment, as he began to tell me about his mother, who was very ill. She had lymphoma, he said, and didn't have long to live. His father had died in a boating accident long before, when he was a teenager.

"I'll be an orphan," he laughed in a weary, hollow way, "a middle-aged orphan."

His mom had given Martin and his sister (who lived near her in Seattle) some cash for Christmas. Might as well have some of it now, she'd said in a note, and not wait for the will. She'd packed Martin's money up in a gift box and sent it to him special delivery. It had arrived that day, Martin said, though you weren't supposed to send cash through the mail, so she'd taken a real chance.

"The chemo must have fried her brain," he whispered grimly.

Martin lived on the fourth floor of a graffiti-covered building near the Bowery. An odor of cat piss hit me when we walked through the door of his apartment, my eyes welling up momentarily from the smell, though I never saw a cat. It was a dark and cluttered studio with an unmade futon in the corner, books and papers strewn on all the surfaces, and empty liquor bottles scattered around the kitchen, which was really just a row of appliances lined up against the wall. The mess reminded me of the chaos at home in Pennsylvania. I preferred things streamlined and orderly in my own life. Tess and I actually got along in this regard. Our apartment in Williamsburg wasn't anything palatial, but at least it was clean and neat, which is probably the reason she'd been able to sublet it so fast.

"Sorry about the place," Martin said, making a sweeping gesture toward everything. "Wasn't exactly expecting company."

He sounded slurry again. He went immediately to the freezer and pulled out a bottle of vodka.

"Want a drink?"

"I don't drink," I said, but not as sweetly as I'd said it in the restaurant.

"Oh, that's right. But do you mind if I do?" he asked as he was pouring himself a large glass.

I noticed Martin's hand was shaking. I wondered if he was nervous about my being there or if this was just a byproduct related to the heavy drinking. After growing up with my dad, I could spot someone with a problem a mile away, but Martin wasn't exactly hiding the evidence. We moved to the futon and I looked some more around the room. There was a two-foot, half-decorated Christmas tree on a TV tray near the window. This contributed to the lonely feel of the place. You could see the rest of Martin's life playing out here, and in his short trips to and from the restaurant and his work at the bookstore, where he was apparently still functioning for the time being.

Martin began telling me how handsome I was, how easy I was to talk to. He said he hadn't brought anyone home like this for a long time, which given the bleak surroundings and his obvious issues, might have been true. He'd already downed the vodka and now seemed very drunk, as he began to grope and tug at me, crawling all over me, in fact. His breath was terrible, and his movements were jumpy and awkward. Luckily, because of the state he was in, he wasn't up to much, and I let my mind wander through the rest of it.

I woke up at dawn, the soft winter light streaming through the dirty windows. Martin was out cold. I crossed to the bathroom. I'd made it through the night and now wanted to get out of there as soon as possible, before Martin woke up, before he got any ideas about us hooking up again. It was ugly and depressing there. I'd have to think up another plan for the next evening. I put my clothes on as quietly as I could and went to leave.

The gift box was sitting on a chair near the front door. I hadn't noticed it earlier, but I knew what it was before I lifted its lid. I looked over at Martin, drooling and unzipped on the futon, and thought, quite simply, that he didn't deserve that cash. He'd only drink it up, I told myself. He'd squander it the way my father had squandered all his paychecks and everything else in his life. At least if I took it, I'd be putting it to practical use—by which I meant my own survival. I barely hesitated before reaching in and scooping up the bills. I didn't count them until I was out in the hallway: two thousand dollars. I wasn't worried too much about getting caught. The only thing Martin really knew about me was my work at the answering service, but I hadn't told him which one (there were a ton of these places), and I wasn't even working there anymore. Plus, he didn't have my actual name. I doubted Martin would go to the police. He was a careless drunk who'd been ripped off by a gay hustler. (This was the only way to categorize it.) The cops wouldn't have given him much sympathy or attention for that. Not back then, at least. Everyone would think he deserved what he got.

I needn't have worried about scary silences around the dinner table. It was a talkative crowd. The food stylist, who supervised us all as we'd prepared various aspects of the citrus chicken dinner (he was particularly helpful in the juice reduction stage), told us some secrets from his time photographing food for magazine ads. Some of these I already knew—Elmer's glue in a cereal bowl, mashed potatoes for vanilla ice cream, using spray deodorant to give fruit that "cold sweat" look. He also entertained us with stories from his distant past, when he'd been a porn distributor for a time and had once been held out a tenth-story window by his ankles after running afoul of the mob—a wild story, delivered with such hilarious detail, it had us all rolling. Henry sat next to Joe, and at one point he went on about some copyright issues for a book of lithographs he wanted to publish, picking my husband's brain for free legal advice. Our invitation to the island suddenly made more sense. Then the masseur told us about which celebrities had the best bodies and who had cellulite and who was well-endowed and who was not. This led to more stories about close encounters with movie stars.

Martin, who was at the other end of the table (I'd sat as far away from him as possible and avoided him earlier in the bustling kitchen), told about the time he'd bumped into Tom Cruise rushing for a taxi on

Fifth Avenue, literally knocking him off his feet. Joe told an appealing story I'd heard a hundred times, about striking up a conversation with Molly Ringwald, as she stood behind him in the checkout line at a Food Emporium. Then, after that, Joe turned to me and told me I should mention the celebrities I'd spoken with at the answering service. I thought I felt Martin turn his gaze in my direction, some heightened interest, but I was careful to avoid any eye contact and couldn't really be sure. The food stylist didn't wait for me to respond. He was already laughing, mentioning a Ryan Gosling look-alike at his steam room, and then the conversation took on another tone entirely.

"You were quiet tonight," Joe said.

Dinner was over and so was the cleanup. Now we were in our room, getting ready for bed. The room was large and comfortable, with Hockney prints on the cream-colored walls and an ivory duvet covering the king-sized bed.

"Was I?" I said. "Tough competition, I guess. Lose your breath, you lose your turn."

"Rare for you to be so quiet," Joe replied with his trademark concern.

"Are you going to be able to help Henry?" I asked, changing the subject.

"I don't know. I told him to send me the documents on Monday."

"Well, now we know why we got invited."

"Hey, look, he could have just called me on the phone, Nate. At least we're getting a weekend out of it."

My husband's upbeat spin was something I'd come to count on through the years.

"True," I said, and then Joe kissed me good night and turned out the lamp beside the bed.

When I'd left Martin's place that morning, it was still very early, but I figured I should walk in the direction of Port Authority and pick up my stuff. Then maybe I'd find a cheap hotel, some place with a weekly rate. I was going to have to be careful with expenses, but at least I wasn't panicked anymore. I kept touching the cash in my pocket. When I was just past Washington Square Park, I saw one of the operators from the answering service coming toward me on the sidewalk. We greeted each other warmly (two early-morning wanderers), though we barely spoke to each other at work. I'm not even sure if he knew I'd been fired. He was a straight guy named Finch who mostly kept to himself. Now on the street he was telling me he was quitting the service and moving to London. He was leaving his bombed-out apartment in the East Village where he lived with three other guys. His spot there was up for grabs, and so I took it, moving in right away.

Later, one of these roommates would recommend me as a server for his brother's catering company in Chelsea, doing deliveries, cleaning the kitchen, working my way up. A couple of months into the job, I had to go to a law firm in midtown where I was shown into a conference room. I had to unpack sandwiches and put everything on a table for a luncheon. I lost my grip on a coffee urn and the coffee spilled everywhere. The office manager and one of the secretaries kept screaming at me while I was down on the carpet trying to soak up the spill with napkins. A good-looking associate (whose parents owned a sandwich shop, as it turned out) came barreling in with paper towels from the men's room. He kneeled down next to me and helped me clean up the mess as we traded shy smiles. This, of course, was Joe.

His reflexive kindness that day got my attention. It was something I wasn't used to. And then, once we started going out (he'd come back to the conference room later and written his phone number on my wrist, a rom-com gesture, when I was packing everything up), he watched me with such determined optimism; it was as if he was willing some better version of me to the surface. It took me a while to realize this was how Joe watched everyone, how he basically looked at the whole world and me in particular. This knowledge only seemed to make him more irresistible. I did try to become a better person, more or less. I worked hard to justify Joe's blind faith in me anyway. Meeting Joe was like being caught up in the current of a river. This was one way to explain it, as corny as it sounds. I was swept along anyway—into marriage and parenthood and to the suburbs, happily for the most part, if you don't count that affair and a few other petty, stupid complaints.

I couldn't sleep, so I got up, threw on some shorts and a T-shirt, and walked quietly through the beach house. I took the spiral staircase up to the roof. There was a party going on next door, at the home of the beautiful boys, music flooding through the speakers and a surge of laughter echoing in the darkness. I stood watching the summer sky, which was mostly overcast that night. The ocean rippled like a black sheet in the distance.

I didn't notice him right away. Then I was aware of some movement to my left. He was sitting in one of the Adirondack chairs. I saw the ember of the cigarette he was holding first, glowing in the dark. Henry had signs up all over the place—*If you're smoking, you had better be on fire,* so Martin was flouting the rule and taking a chance.

"I'm sorry," I said. "I didn't know anyone was up here."

"I didn't mean to startle you," Martin replied.

He put the cigarette out then, got up, and walked over to me.

"It's you. Isn't it?"

I didn't say anything. I kept staring out toward the ocean.

"I had an inkling," he continued. "But I wasn't sure until tonight, when Joe mentioned the answering service. Do you mind me saying I would never have recognized you?"

"I've changed, I guess."

"Yes, you have. You were very handsome once."

"I remember you, though," I said.

"Do you?"

"Yes. I do."

We stood there for a minute without saying anything else. Whitney Houston's "So Emotional" was playing next door, loud and jubilant, as if it were still decades ago.

"You didn't ruin my life or anything, Nate," Martin said now. "Or should I say Caleb?"

"I'm glad to hear it," I said, "that I didn't ruin your life."

"You weren't important enough to do that. You weren't even important enough to get me sober. It took another three years and more messed-up behavior for that to happen."

He chuckled tiredly.

I didn't know what to say. An apology didn't seem to be what he was after. And I wasn't sure I could pull off the sincerity of it anyway.

"I assume Joe doesn't know. No worries there. This isn't a blackmail thing. I won't tell him or Henry either, for that matter, though I think Henry's heard the story before, in our twelve-step meetings, when I've shared how some hustler ripped me off one Christmas while my mother was dying."

I stayed silent as Martin moved toward the stairs.

"I wouldn't mind getting the two-thousand dollars back," he said without turning around to look at me. "It might be a way you can exercise a little generosity of spirit, something you didn't possess in your youth. But it will have to be up to you. You know where to find me. Good night, Nate."

And then he was gone.

I stayed on the roof. It was quieter now across the way. The party was either winding down or had moved inside. I believed Martin when he said he wouldn't tell Joe. I assumed this was somehow tied in with his sobriety and his twelve-step work, some notion of personal forgiveness I couldn't quite wrap my head around. He certainly could have been crueler to me or angrier, something beyond telling me I had aged badly. I might not even have to give back the two thousand dollars. I'd have to think about that part.

Before I went downstairs and crawled back into bed with Joe, I remembered something from years before, back when my affair had ended with that dad from Ellie's school. I hadn't been the one to end it. Whenever I tried to, it didn't take. I referred to our frequent reconciliations as relapses, not always in jest. I didn't love this guy. It was more like a pigheaded yearning, a mulish lust. We'd been taking more and more risks as the affair went on. It was only a matter of time before we'd be found out, and then I'd be exposed as the fraud that I was—a faithless husband; a languid, selfish parent. How my mindless narcissism might have done us all in. Then this man, my lover, had come to me with the news that he was taking a job in North Carolina, mostly to get away from me. He was moving there with his family. His wife was pregnant again. I remember conjuring a reaction of grief and distress when he told me he was leaving, but the truth was that I was filled with nothing but relief, because it had all been taken out of my hands. It felt like the other lucky times in my life, when suddenly, out of nowhere, I'd been saved.

ACKNOWLEDGMENTS

I am deeply grateful to Drue Heinz and her amazing legacy. The impact of her tireless support of writers and the literary arts cannot be overstated.

There isn't anyone on the planet who wouldn't be better off after reading the work of Manuel Muñoz. My fandom stops just short of the restraining-order category, so I will always be a little in disbelief that he chose my collection for the Drue Heinz Literature Prize. I cannot thank him enough.

I am so grateful to the gifted Caroline Kim, for her generous support and kindness.

Many thanks to Mitchell Waters, my remarkable agent and friend, whose loyal presence in my life has made such a difference.

To Miriam Clark, an early reader of most of these stories, for her keen intelligence and guidance, and to Denise Tolan, for her talent, encouragement and infectious enthusiasm.

Thank you to the wonderfully talented team at the University of Pittsburgh Press, whose expertise and hard work have helped bring this book into the world. It has been a true pleasure working with them: Jane McCafferty, Alex Wolfe, Kelly Lynn Thomas, Christine Ma, Deborah Orgel Hudson, Lesley Rains, and Caleb Gill.

I wish to thank the editors of the publications where earlier versions of these stories were published: *Willow Springs* ("If You Only Knew"), *december* ("Off the Grid"), *Chicago Quarterly Review* ("The World at Large"), *Solstice* ("Unlike Some People"), *Emerald City* ("The Disaster Book"), *South Carolina Review* ("Certain Healing Properties"), *Iron Horse Literary Review* ("Little Bandits"), and Bold Strokes Books' *Saints+Sinners: New Fiction from the Festival 2021* ("The Lost Object Exercise").

A special thank you to David Leavitt, a literary hero of mine, who originally published the title story, "A Place in the World," in his great magazine, *Subtropics*. His generosity and encouragement have meant more to me than I can say.

It has been a long road to this collection. Most of these stories were written in the middle of the night or on the subway commuting to my various jobs over the years. One early story here was begun as I cradled my then infant son (who was the happiest of babies, but a reluctant sleeper) while I typed with one hand at 3:00 a.m. In other words, writers figure out a way to get the work done, and the rest is a combination of persistence, blind faith, and hopefully a thick skin. It also helps to have a little luck. I've had much more than that, thanks to my incredible family and friends.

To the following, who buoyed me in countless ways with their love and support while I was writing these stories, whether they realized it or not: Martha Gaythwaite and John Tebbetts, Susan and John Loftus, Meg Loftus Suchan and Shaun Suchan, Jack Tebbetts, Bill Tebbetts, Kim Harris, Naomi May, Joel May, Julian May, Simon Donovan, Judd Stark and Jeremy Walker, Denise and Matthew Price, Donald Albrecht, Burt Brody, Michael Fishman, Regina McFadden, Kevin Meade, Veronique Jeanmarie, and Elaine Stenson.

And to Connor, Julia, John, Julian, Catherine, Alexandra, Josh, Jayvin, Jurnee, and Jream, in case they ever want to read this book some time in the future to see what I was up to.

To my parents, who were voracious readers and hilarious storytellers, and who taught me by example every day.

To my son, Zach, who was often the first person with whom I shared any positive publishing news and whose reactions were always a kick.

And to Tommy, who astonishes every day with his love, patience, and creativity. Thank you—for literally everything. Yep, to have you with me (as Julie Andrews sang), *I must have done something good*.

Finally, without Katherine Mosby's stunning support and encouragement from the moment I walked into her workshop at the 92nd Street Y, this book would not have been possible. It's as simple as that.